THE AMERICAS

P J SEARLE

to all free Americans…

iUniverse, Inc.
Bloomington

The Americas

iUniverse books may be ordered through booksellers or by contacting:

iUniverse
1663 Liberty Drive
Bloomington, IN 47403
www.iuniverse.com
1-800-Authors (1-800-288-4677)

Because of the dynamic nature of the Internet, any web addresses or links contained in this book may have changed since publication and may no longer be valid. The views expressed in this work are solely those of the author and do not necessarily reflect the views of the publisher, and the publisher hereby disclaims any responsibility for them.

Any people depicted in stock imagery provided by Thinkstock are models, and such images are being used for illustrative purposes only.

Certain stock imagery © Thinkstock.

ISBN: 978-1-4620-0081-4 (sc)
ISBN: 978-1-4620-0082-1 (ebook)

Printed in the United States of America

iUniverse rev. date: 3/10/2011

Foreword

As the song lyric states, "*This* is not America." This fiction is set in an imaginary United States—a USA that now includes, through mutual annexation, the whole of Canada.

Set in modern-day USA, 'The Americas' is an amalgam of ancient democracy and archaic European feudalism—or for want of a better analogy, medieval USA.

Rather than imaginary, 'The Americas' could be seen as a time-slip—a glimpse into a parallel universe—a *temporal loop* in which time runs normally for a set period but then skips back, like a cracked record to a time past, and then continues on, adding fuel to the old adage: 'History repeats itself.'

Though a study in miniature (viewed through the glass darkly), America still shines out, but not *quite* as we know it.

P J Searle

Book One

'Men at some time are masters of their fates:
the fault, dear Brutus, is not in our stars,
but in ourselves, that we are underlings.'
—Julius Cæsor

I

The twin-engine props suddenly whined, and the aircraft yawed and dipped.

Ex-US President Pooley instinctively held the armrest of his seat in forlorn hope of steadying the craft. "Damn!" he cried out, as if someone had done it purposely to spite him. "I hate turbulence. Go tell the pilot to fly above it, will you, Joe? Makes my stomach churn. And tell him to put the heating up. Feels like someone's left the goddamn back gate open."

Joe, the younger of Pooley's two aides, got up and—without showing frustration or contempt—walked down the aircraft toward the pilot's cabin. Halfway along, something caught his eye in the approaching morning light. As he looked toward the earth below, a shadow momentarily passed the last porthole. He paused and peered out into the vaporous cloud.

In the Presidential suite of the Lexicon hotel, Brazil, morning had also broken. It was the same continent, but a different morning. From a similar vaporous cloud, US President-elect Janus Shar emerged from his shower. His once six-foot stature had, over the past decade, lost a few inches to rounding shoulders, making him look much older than his mere sixty years. Entering the second half of his third and last term, the crushing burden of office had—though he'd never admit it to himself or anyone else—taken its toll.

Lazily he pulled on a bathrobe and made his way to the adjoining bedroom, stopping on the way to pick up a newspaper from a pile. He scanned the headline as he approached the king-size bed where a beautiful young woman, Cloirina Braganza, lay sleeping.

He woke her with a kiss and the mildest of rebukes, "Another fine mess you got me into," he whispered into her ear. "So, how you feeling this morning?"

Cloirina opened one eye: a jet-black orb set in flawless pearl blinked into consciousness. "I'm fine," she replied. "And how are you today?"

"As always, Honey, just doodle-dandy," he said, adding his famous complimentary wink.

Cloirina's other eye sprang open as she suddenly remembered something. "Oh! You are leaving today. I don't want you to go." She sighed deeply as she wiped the corner of her eye. "And don't leave it too long before you come back or I'll come to your White House and get you myself—okay?"

"Sure, sure. Don't worry," he said, enjoying her girlish chide. "You seen this shit your *gutter* press is saying about us?"

"Don' swear … it's not nice."

He smiled at her, but she did not smile back. He shook the newspaper toward her and read the quote. "'Most beautiful woman in the world and the most powerful man in the world in love nest.' Jesus, love *nest*."

"And *don't* blaspheme. I read it. So?"

Shar smiled again. "So, with your looks and my brains, some fancy offspring we'd make in this *love nest*. I forget who said that."

"Albert Einstein to Marilyn Monroe," Cloirina said, "and she supposedly answered, 'But with your looks and my brains, we'd make an ugly idiot' … something like that. And we *are* making an offspring as you call it. I can feel our child, now, moving in my belly."

"Stomach …" said Shar. "I hate the word belly."

She gave him an incredulous stare. "We are also running out of time—" She stopped abruptly, feeling a sudden flood of nausea, put her hand to her mouth and gagged.

"You okay?" said Shar placing a reassuring hand on her shoulder.

"Sure … no! Not so doodle-dandy."

Shar looked down at her. Even holding back a mouthful of puke, she was beautiful. "Christ. You sure it's too late?"

She swallowed. "I said *don't* blaspheme."

"Sorry. You don't look no three months to me."

"Well, you better believe it. And *this* time is for keeps. Your precious Senate need not know until the amendment is made. Don't spill your beans before you get them to market."

"You know—you're not as dumb as you look."

"You think I look dumb?"

"Yeah, in a sexy sort of way… Darling."

"Just you understand this," she hissed, turning on him like a scolding mother to a naughty child, and adding a cutting edge to her voice. "When you marry into this family, the connection will be fused. You get the heiress to the richest and most influential family in Brazil. My dowry *is* Brazil—the gateway to the whole of South America—from Guatemala to Tierra del Fuego." Her chastisement vented, her voice now softened a decibel. "And what do I get in return? A stupid-looking old man with skinny, bandy legs. Pretty good bargain for you, yes, *Darling*?"

"Hey! Them's *Texas* legs you're talking about. And in that bargain, I could end up buying the goddamn Ponderosa—just like Pooley."

"I told you not to blaspheme … how many times? What we are about—we will need God on our side."

Shar shrugged and walked back to the bathroom, the door opening to another cloud of steam.

Truman Pilgrim Pooley had been, as the latter part of his middle name suggested, grim. Not a pleasant word but, regrettably, apt. During his Presidential election campaign, some sixteen years and four Presidential terms earlier, the opposition had, somewhat prosaically, tagged he and his elder brother, Silus—whose middle name was also Pilgrim (a family tradition due to their connection to the first settlers)—the Brothers Grim. Little good it did the attempts to scuttle his Presidential bid, for the Pooley connection with the amalgamation known infamously as the three M's—Mormons, Mafia, and Masons—plus a humongous family fortune and the treacherous, inherent nature essential for amassing and securing such, left the opposition little chance. Truman P. Pooley, in spite of all his many failings, had been elected President *courtesy* of the three M's: money, money, and then more money.

No one was over surprised, or seemed too disturbed, when Silus P. Pooley was ignobly slain in scandalous circumstances two years into his brother's disastrous presidency. Through neglect and, as some said, downright recalcitrance, the Pooley regime had dragged America virtually into the hands of the receiver. The dollar, along with world standing and the American can-do spirit, had plummeted to an all time low; America had entered its own Dark Age. So when Pooley's one and only term had finally run its crooked course, there was a universal sigh of relief. The election had not been about who would win, but how much the opposition candidate, Janus Shar, would win *by*. Subsequently, the landslide victory was openly quoted in the press as "the understatement of the last four grueling years." America, and indeed the whole world, thanked God, Yahweh, Jehovah, Allah, lucky stars, the number 8, and whoever or whatever else they prayed to, for deliverance.

As for the reviled Truman P. Pooley, his only saving grace had been his trade venture with Brazil, a venture in which, eighteen years on, he was still an active player. On that fateful day, he sat in his private aircraft flying over the Brazilian interior working on his forthcoming speeches, assisted by two aides. As he scanned the many documents before him, he suddenly balked at an offending phrase.

"Jesus! How did this line get in here: *Unification of The Americas?* How many times I got to tell you people, your Brazilian politician likes his business like his women—up-front and simple. I'm trying to sell entry to a trade deal—not a goddamn yacht race. *Am I right, or am I right?*"

Riceman, the older of the two aides, pushed his glasses up his nose and screwed his eyes in frustration. "Give them some credit, Sir; they know what it is. We think it should stay."

"*You* think it should stay?"

"Yes, Sir," said the aide. "It's our only USP."

"The hell it is! *I'm* the unique selling proposition, me, T.P. Pooley—that name still means something, and I didn't get where I am today by giving goddamn *credit!* And who in hell gives a rat's ass what *you* think? The Americas is a Shar thing. I hate it—take it out. We won't have this conversation again, am I right?"

"Yes, no, Sir," Riceman said. "I'll take it out."

At the other end of the aircraft, Joe stared out of the last porthole toward the nebula cloud formation. He watched for a moment, but whatever he'd seen was now long-gone. He shook away the troublesome thought and continued through to the cabin. The aircraft was still buffeting slightly, he assumed from turbulence. It didn't particularly bother him, but T.P. Pooley called the shots. He opened the cabin door and peered in. The cockpit was completely *empty*. Without showing shock or panic, he turned—his ingrained instinct was to warn Pooley—but realizing the futility of this action, he instead entered the cabin, slipped quickly into the pilot's seat, and grabbed the stick—to no avail. The mountain range ahead was too close; it loomed up with perilous speed.

The neon mirror-light flickered to life, illuminating Janus Shar's face as he began to shave.

Cloirina called to him from the bedroom, continuing their conversation. "The air-crash investigation indicated pilot error," she said defensively.

"That so?" he called back through a face of shaving lather. "The official findings said *open verdict*. Some reckon I—"

"Pooley was Brazil's premature wedding gift," she called louder. "Their show of good faith."

"The hell do you mean?" Shar charged back into the bedroom, angrily wiping shaving lather from his face. "You're not suggesting—?"

"I know you didn't want it; *I* never wanted it. Pooley was set against this union; he was not a visionary. *Brazil* wanted it. Some say it was rebels, Chad; some say your CIA. But it was Brazil."

"Yeah, well, back home they blame *me*."

She moved to him, kissed his soapy cheek, and smiled maternally. "There, there, no one blames you, *Meester Presiden*."

"Goddamn it! I murdered him at the ballot box—he hadn't been a threat for fifteen years. I didn't need that. Why?"

"Who knows why, Janus? Because he still had *influence*, who knows? Brazil *needs* this union. I can sway the rest. Once all Brazil comes over, Argentina, Chile, and the rest will follow. Colombia is already … how you say in my *purse?* And Bolivia—whose namesake, Simon Bolivar, dreamed of a United States of South America— he'd been a great admirer of the American fight for independence. It too is in my purse"

"Pocket."

"*Whichever.* This is what I bring to our marriage, and our child will inherit … that's your part of it. You promise, yes?"

"Hey, I ain't divorced yet … you're forgetting BB."

"That frigid bitch won't stand in our way. Can she give you a child? Can she give you The Americas? You *promise,* yes?"

"Okay, okay! Jesus Christ, Cloirina!"

"You will *not* blaspheme in my presence. How many times I tell you?"

"Okay, okay! Look, Betty won't stand in our way. Everything is right on course. Canada is about to finalize … Maxwell Tunney's work. Who'd have thought the Brits and French would have done a deal? Money, money, money." He shook his head sagely. "See, the British gave away their empire … just *gave* it away. They'd forgotten how greedy the rest of the world was. One empire falls, another rises." He paused and considered. Cloirina gestured with a raised eyebrow for him to continue. "Okay, this Americas union will raise the dollar back to number one. And, as you say, we are running out of time. I need that extension. They know I won't commit without it; they *must* grant it. *And* they will! They'll do anything to get their greedy mitts on these Southern Territories."

"We want more than that. What we want is—" She suddenly gagged, and again grabbed at her stomach. "I think I'm gonna throw up."

"Hell, no! Don't do that. I hate that." Shar helped her off the bed, trying to hide the look of disgust on his face. "How can you do something so goddamn vile?"

She gagged again, quickly putting her hands to her mouth in a vain attempt to stop the inevitable. The viscous slime voided through her fingers and splattered her naked feet and the priceless woven carpet beneath.

Shar turned his head away, picked up the phone, and barked into the mouthpiece. "Get in here, will you? And bring a domestic." He turned back to her. "You okay, Honey? I have to go—I've got Tunney waiting in the annexe."

Cloirina, not moving a muscle, stared back at him, bewildered. He, likewise, not knowing what to do next, and, like a drowning man giving up the struggle, he slipped instinctively into his defense mechanism, thinking, *Okay, this ain't really happening to me.*

After a few moments, a flurry of aides streamed in, fussing around the beautiful, puke-smeared heiress, directing her into the bathroom.

Shar bowed theatrically and gave his famous wink that the world had come to understand, invariably preceded one of his cliché catchphrases.

"What you see … is what you get," he chuckled as he ducked out of the room.

II

The US Vice President, Maxwell Tunney, waited nervously in the Lexicon hotel, Presidential suite, annexe. He was not looking forward to this meeting, since the press had all but said that Max had fucked up. In truth, he hadn't. *He* had brought Canada into the negotiation arena and into the USA proper. But it was Shar, with the promise of a share in the new Southern Territories, who had clinched the deal. Max didn't crave glory. He was, due to his high birth, a player in this hierarchy, but he was *not* ambitious. Everything he had ever achieved had been handed to him on a silver plate. He looked good in a suit—handsome, debonair. Max was the man to send to pacify a troublesome meeting, which he could do simply by turning up. He was the tinsel, the decoration on the Presidential Christmas tree. But all Max had ever wanted was to serve his friend and President, Janus Shar.

At length, Shar entered. "Max!" he yelled, grabbing him in a hug, "Nice of you to turn out. You ready to hand back the reins?"

"Sure as hell am, J?" said Max with a sigh of relief. He had been expecting a rebuff, but Shar's well-met humor had taken him somewhat by surprise. Max smiled and returned the hug, "It's like sticking your bare ass into a hornet's nest. I didn't do too good, did I?"

"You did just fine, Max, just fine."

"Hey, for *reins,* read *reigns*, get it … joke?" Max laughed—Shar did not. "They've all but sanctioned it. If they offer, will you take it?

"No!"

"*No?* Well, I *am* offering it, J—the opportunity to stand for an extra term in office. With 80 percent of the vote, it's a mere formality … now or never. They'll go along with Cloirina, but they won't like the child. Take it before she starts to show."

"No."

Max slapped his hands to his head in exasperation. "Jesus H. Christ, J, this is the only thing I was able to do for you. They're ready; *it's* ready … for the taking."

Shar smiled, pulled down one of Max's hands, and spoke directly into his Vice President's ear. "Not like this, Max. I want more. I want it offered from the *other* side."

"You shouldn't joke about it, J."

"I'm not joking, Max. Them sons-of-bitches will have to beg me … *and* they will. The Americas … when I offer them that, they'll give me anything."

"Well, you've earned it J. It's … destiny. The unification of The Americas—God, that sounds good."

"Yeah, sounds historic! I want it *hereditary*."

The statement hung in the air; it visibly shocked Max and he was unable to stop his face showing it.

Shar turned on him with damning eyes. "Listen to me, Max: If I'm to commit my family's fortune to this venture—and more—I *need* that protection. When I'm gone—without a Shar in office—the family will never get it back. You don't think I deserve it?"

Max shrugged. "Jesus!"

"You'd better be sure of yourself, Maxwell. I need to know my team is with me on this hereditary issue. It need only be for a single generation—until the debt's repaid. How say?"

Max forced an unconvincing laugh, desperate to give a display of loyalty and solidarity. "Hell, J, you just took me somewhat by surprise. But *they* won't like it— and that's a fact. Christ, will they not. We are talking virtual monarchy."

Shar stared overlong at his Vice President. "Dynasty—not monarchy." He asked again, this time with menace. "How *say*?"

"J, it goes without saying." Max was decidedly uncomfortable. "Haven't I been your strongest ally? Your confidant through the conglomerate wars? Instrumental in the defeat of President Pooley? Confederate in the long, and sometimes dirty, struggle for the presidency? That's what your own memoirs said."

"You forgot one quote: 'For Maxwell Tunney's loyalty, I duly nominate him Vice President.' Now, I need you to commit!"

"I'm with you, J. I'm with you … like always."

Shar shook his head to Max's feeble show of commitment. "Some didn't like the fact that you were

Canadian born." There was now a hint of contempt in his voice. "Some said the job was just too big for you—that you were a free spirit, liked to play: wine, women, and more goddamn women—some said. But I pay my dues, Max, so don't cross me on this." His face softened into a smile, "Just watch your ass, boy."

Max also smiled, with relief. "Yeah, and you watch *your* ass, tomorrow."

"You mean the Senate? You're still jet-lagging, Max—that's the day *after* tomorrow."

"No, J. I mean tomorrow—the press conference at the airport. They know about Cloirina. You've trashed the people's darling."

Shar manufactured a smile. "That reminds me, Max. You can do me a great personal service. When you get back stateside, go see BB for me. Tell her ... tell her the Cloirina thing was no more than political bonding. And the baby, just rumor ... not mine. Tell her we didn't even ... well, you'll think of something; you've done it before. You know Betty better than I do myself—you're the ladies man. Just make it right."

Max caught his breath; he was shocked and now sickened. He gave Shar a questioning look, but loyally nodded, mumbling a grudging, "If I must. But, *what* about Cloirina ... the child?"

"The hell is wrong with you, Max? I ain't about to lose BB for some goddamn adolescent. She knew what she was up to. I got what I needed: the will of the people."

"God, you can't mean that?"

"Look, the ball's rolling and no love child is going to jeopardize it. Money, money, money—that's what's talking now. I need them both sweet, Max—until *both* sides of the house comply."

"Is that all she means to you?"

Shar gave Max an incredulous look. "God sakes— grow up. You're supposed to be a man of the world. How many affairs have you had?"

Max didn't relish this conversation. If he won, he lost. And if he lost … "Let's move on. We've got higher priorities."

"You think that? My main priority now is BB. Go see her, Max. Make it right, Mr. Vice President of all The Americas. You can do it … for me. Do it for *me*. Tell the First Lady I want to come home, rip the divorce papers up, and … just pave the way. Christ, you know the sort of things to say, you know BB well enough — you've done it before. You know the sort of words she likes to hear. I need the American people behind me on this one, Maxwell." He raised an eyebrow, making the statement into a question. He could tell Max was weakening. "What do you say?"

Max gave an inward sigh of defeat. "Okay, okay. When the President tells Tunney to do something, it's done. See you in DC … in two days." Janus smiled, winked, and walked out.

Max Tunney stared through the porthole of his private aircraft at the setting sun, deliberating his unwelcome chore. Various aides attempted to engage him in business-of-the-day conversation, to no avail. He made it clear that he wanted to be alone with his thoughts.

At Pooley International Airport, Washington DC (the Pooley name having stuck due to the fact the family estate still held tenancy on the land), those same thoughts were with Max as he entered his limousine. Max had always had a way with women, to a point—that point being the trivial conversations of the libertine seducer. He was no good at intrigue and had always avoided adulterous liaisons wherever possible. So where did that leave him now? He could use a drink. Should he stop for some dutch courage or …? The notion was quickly resolved as the limousine turned into the driveway of Blue Haven, Betty Shar's opulent Washington mansion.

Max got wearily out of the limousine, dismissed his chauffeur and aide, and walked alone to the entrance. A woman servant ushered him into the palatial morning room where Betty Shar—a petite brunette of forty-five and bearing more than a passing resemblance to the cartoon character, Betty Boop (hence the nick-name, BB)—sat primly on a two-seat sofa at a small table, pouring tea. She spoke without looking up.

"Come in, Maxwell." She then smiled up at the servant. "Thank you, Rose. We don't want to be disturbed for an hour … for anything." The servant smiled and backed out of the door. Betty went back to pouring tea.

Max stood for a moment, not quite knowing what to do next. He reminded himself that he'd always avoided this deviousness. So, how come he found himself in this mess?

"Tea, Mr. Vice President?" Betty Shar now looked up from the table and offered a cup. "Wakey, wakey, Maxwell."

Max could not help his voice sounding curt. "No, thank you," he growled, wishing the ground would swallow them both up.

BB smiled her bespoke smile as she imitated his gruff tone. "*No, thank you.* Sit by me, Max. I promise I won't bite."

He crossed the room in three long strides and sat as close to her as he could without actually making contact. Betty twisted on the cushion as if to make herself more comfortable.

She smiled a different smile now as she spoke—an intimate smile. "Hmm, my boy is frisky today. It's been a long time—"

Max stifled her mouth with a passionate kiss, and grabbed at her tiny breast, almost spilling the tea.

"He wants to come home," he blurted as he pulled away. "Lover-boy, damn him, wants to come home."

It was the manufactured smile again as Betty responded. "He always wants to come home … after. You know him; this has happened a hundred times. He has a little bit of fun, *then* … he wants to come home."

"And that's okay? You said it was finished this time. I never would have—"

"I truly believed it was, Max. I truly did."

"But he can't act that way; he's the President, for Christ's sake!"

"Oh, he's much more than that, *isn't* he, Maxwell? I know he's confided in you … the Great Game." She gave him an all-knowing look.

Max felt decidedly uneasy. Betty appeared better informed of Shar's ambitions than he was. "Don't call me Maxwell," he said with an edge to his voice. "People always call me that when they're about to dump on me. And don't look at me like that. Believe me, I'm no part of this *Great Game*."

Betty smiled. He didn't smile back. She stood up, ran her hands down her shapely thighs, straightening her tight, short skirt, and then walked to the middle of the room. She spoke without looking at him.

"I do believe you, Max, but he knows he can't go it alone. He needs *you*, and he needs *me*, and America needs *him*. I know what I'd prefer, Darling. I'm looking at it now. But I won't play the game his way this time. That I promise."

"So, this is a game to you, too?"

"I know this may sound corny as Kansas, Max, but I'm in love with a wonderful guy. There'll be time for us."

"You deserve better, BB." His brooding anger now subsided. "You gave him everything. He just takes, takes … goddamn it, why the hell is he like that? It was his fault that *we* started this. Him sending me to you every time he wanted to find favor—for me to make it right, to smooth things over. What has he made me?"

She sat down, reached for his hand, and studied his face. He was in torment, torn betwixt loyalties. She stood and led him into the adjoining rest room.

Max sat on the great bed and studied her as she undressed. She was, as the many magazines and tabloids constantly declared, uniquely beautiful. Her naturally jet-black hair, blue eyes, powder-white, flawless skin, and bee-sting breasts, her... God sake, this was driving him to madness. He had to think of something else, a diversion.

"What about us?" he asked, more to break the silence than to get a real answer—he knew the answer only too well. "Where does this leave me? I always thought we'd—"

She closed his lips with a long, elegant finger. "Poor, poor Max. We must all make the sacrifice—do our bit for *king* and country."

He buried his head in her naked breast. Was he actually crying? If he was, he didn't want her to know—*he* didn't want to know.

The avenue to Brazil's International Airport was lined ten-deep with people. A convoy of black limousines swept by, security men running alongside, their eyes burning into the cheering crowd who were waving both US and Brazilian flags. News-sellers offered their wares, shrieking out their particular tabloid's headline:

"Shar & Stripes for Brazil."

"Twinkle, Twinkle, Little Shar."

"Shar & Clio, And Baby Makes Three-O!"

The limousines came to a halt outside the airport's VIP conference hall, where a myriad of journalists, TV presenters, aides, and photographers were mustered.

A representative called for order, and then gave a spirited, Latin-style introduction. "Ladies and gentlemen, and all people south of Panama: The man, the myth, and now the legend... *Il Presidente* of the United States of America—from Alaska through Canada and down to Panama." He gave a knowing smile. "That is, for the present—Janus Shar!"

A mixed reception greeted President Shar as he was ushered to the lectern. Before he had a chance to speak, a voice boomed out.

"How would you describe your visit to our country, Mr. President?"

Shar turned into the microphones and cameras, unconvincingly offering a face of contrived disappointment. He spoke slowly, exaggerating his Texan drawl. "I am *very* disappointed. I came to this continent with a pocket full o' stars." He made as if to pull a star from his pocket. "And looky here, I still got one left."

The whole room laughed. In the midst of the laughter, another voice called out, mimicking Cloirina's shrill voice. "Who you gonna pin it on, *Meester Presiden?*"

Shar ignored the obvious gibe. "Well, I thought I might offer it to Old Nick." He chuckled into the microphones. "Better a devil you know, right? What do you say to that, Nicaragua?"

More laughter, over which a warning voice called out, "You are running out of time, Shar. Beware them Mid-term blues."

Shar turned to the direction of the voice. "Blues! You crazy? I ain't had the blues since I got here—your hospitality's seen to that."

Another voice called out. "What you pinned on Cloirina, *Meester Presiden?*"

Shar manufactured a face of sincerity. "Why, I pinned on my heart. Oh, yeah, you really got me this time. I'm leaving this old heart of mine behind … but I'll be back for it … and for Cloirina."

The voice came back. "What's the First Lady going to say to that, Mr. President?"

"That lady will wish me well." Shar gave a quizzical look toward the voice. "I make no secret about my affairs." He did a theatrical double take, quickly qualifying the last statement. "Hey, I don't mean those sort of affairs. I never was much of a lover-boy. You all know BB kicked me out nigh on a year ago." More laughter. "Yeah, yeah, I deserved it, I know—she's a beautiful woman and I guess I neglected her for the job. BB don't take too kindly to neglect. The American people allowed us to divorce, which is nisi—absolute in one month. So … I'll be back, that *is* of course, if Cloirina will have me. But BB and I are still good friends. Next question."

From beyond the newspeople and gathered crowd, a young man dressed in battle fatigues thrust his way forward. "Hey, Shar! You looking to be king?"

The crowd was shocked into silence; Shar was momentarily lost for words.

He studied the crowd for the face, then finding his voice, called out: "Is that the press? You don't have to shout at me. What publication are you?"

"I ain't no stinking press. I'm Chico Pasad—the people know me as Chad. Now, are you gonna be king?"

"Well, *Chad*, no way!" said Shar, quickly recovering his dignity. "America don't have kings no more. Not since a long, long while ago." He gave a nod and turned away. "Next question."

"How about dictator?" Chad spat back.

Shar scanned the crowd, not quite making out where the voice had come from. Security, however, had. They pushed their way toward the young man. Chad saw them coming and made a hasty retreat, leaving Shar to answer the hanging, portentous question.

Shar theatrically scratched his head as if such a prospect had never been contemplated. "Dictator, you say?" he said with as much humility as he could summon. "Well, as I understand it, a dictator *dictates. I* do what the hell I'm told… so you'd be better asking the American people—that's *all* the American people. Next question."

A friendly voice this time: "What's planned for the rest of your day, Mr. President?"

Shar took a deep breath of relief. "Today, I start my star-studded whistle-stop visits to Colombia, Panama, and Nicaragua—with a stopover in Mexico. I'm thinking of sponsoring a Wetback, Swim the Rio Grande Gala. What do you say, New NewMexico, you good old boys up for that?" Howls of laughter. "Then I'm going back to USA, to DC, and dinner with BB … sounds like alphabet soup, don't it? Anyone here attended one of BB's Blue Haven dinners?"

Various voices responded.

"I have."

"Yeah, once."

"Me too."

Shar smiled, "Was it good?" He continued without waiting for the obvious answer, "You betcha it was good. Them's the best dinner parties in America, so no way am I plannin' to be late—BB don't take too kindly to lateness. See y'all next time round. Bye now!"

He turned and took a deep breath. Mission accomplished, he moved off, guided through the cheering crowds by an entourage of aides.

Outside the conference hall, a TV news crew scanned the hordes of still-cheering spectators jostling for position along the main road leading back to government house.

The TV anchorman spoke into a handheld microphone. "Hi! Miles Davies here, speaking to you from outside the Jade Palace. Now, if I can make myself heard over this din, I'll try for a comment."

The camera tracked the crowd pressed around the intended spectator. "Sir … Sir? Can I? Sir, this is West Stateside News. Can you give a comment? You speak English?"

Chico Pasad pushed his angry face into the camera lens. "I speak English! The hell you think you are, in the fuquing jungle? *Comment?* I give you comment. We don't need no Shar—and we don't need to be one more stinking star pinned on your God-forgotten flag."

Pasad then melted into the protective crowd. The camera moved on and Davies tried for another spectator. "Sir! Yes. Sir, could you give the American people your opinion? What do you think of President Shar's policy toward the unification of The Americas?" He tipped the microphone toward the chosen spectator. Another protester, Rena Menses, pushed her way in.

"Brazil don't need no American aid—neither does Argentina, nor Chile, nor anywhere south of the Canal. We don' want your blood money, and we don' want your Shar."

Davies turned away without giving comment. He scanned the crowd anxiously until finding his planted spectator.

"Folks, this is Leon Farra. I believe he has a few words for President Shar and the American people."

Farra, a jovial-faced, middle-aged man, eagerly smiled up at the camera. "Hi there, fellow Americans… that is what we are to be … soon, I think…"

III

Air Force One, Shar's Presidential jet, approached Washington DC airport. The distant runway lights had just about conceded their brilliance to the now-rising sun. After an uneventful landing, security procedures and the obligatory pleasantries, Shar and entourage left the VIP lounge to be driven off to the White House. Today would be a busy one. Two meetings, the first of which, with the Senate, would prove the less difficult; his well-laid plans of cabbages and kings were—his whistleblower had reported—successfully leaked, but he would need to tread carefully. The second meeting, with BB, would be, to say the very least, complicated.

The group assembled for the press conference had more than the usual 'Return of President, Debrief' air of expectation. An anticipation of great revelation hung over them; it could be felt, tasted, almost touched. Some stood in groups idly speculating, awaiting his arrival. Others studied the huge Megatron TV screen, replaying continuous highlights of his Brazilian trip. Three men stood apart from the rest: Zachariah Cusac, governor of

New York; Owen Savarge, Mayor of Washington DC; and General Richard Pascalo, head of the Presidential/National Guard. They looked from the screen to one another.

At length, Cusac grimaced and turned from the screen—having seen enough he could contain himself no longer. "What in hell was that about? What's that mother up to?"

Pascalo shrugged. "Who knows, Zack? The man is, after all, a genius."

"The hell he is." Cusac could hardly believe his ears. "The man's a goddamn traitor! You and I both know that, and—"

"Don't put words into my mouth, Governor. If he does manage to haul in Nicaragua, then the rest will follow. If you don't think that's genius, you have … I don't know, strawberry Jell-O for brains."

"Hmmm, I love Jell-O. Your insults are sounding weaker, General. I think you're losing your sense-of-humor. So, you won't speculate?"

"No! I won't speculate."

Savarge looked away from the screen. "How's your knees nowadays, Richard? You get over that old cartilage trouble?"

"What? Well yes, yes, I did. Why'd you ask?"

"Oh, just that you'll be doing a deal of bending soon… front and back … fucking curtsying too, I reckon."

"What are you trying to say, Owen?" Pascalo was livid. "On second thought, just leave me out of your foul-mouthed, petty vendettas." He turned back to the screen.

Half a continent away, a battered, rusted car stopped on the deserted Brazilian street that led to a path of marble colonnaded buildings before the Jade Palace—the state residence of the Braganza dynasty. It was well past curfew; the huge billboard showing a portrait of President Shar was briefly illuminated by the car's interior light as Chad stepped out onto the sidewalk. He quickly shut the door and the street was once again in darkness. Only pale moonlight lit the poster as he pasted a banner over the main slogan that simply said, "The Americas."

Chad stood back for a moment studying his handiwork. The banner now read, "No Shar for Brazil! Viva the Republic!"

He climbed back into the car. Rena Menses, at the wheel, smiled and gave him a mocking, American GI salute. Chad smiled back. They continued on to another poster, then another, posting banners.

A police patrol car, lights extinguished, entered from one end of the street. Another arrived at the far end. Then, from the only side street, a third slowly nosed in effectively blocking any possible escape route. Rena's eyes widened in fear as all sets of car lights came on together.

"Come on, Richard," said Savarge with disbelief. "Don't give me that patriot shit. You *want* the big job—and Shar's about to queer it. He's a wild hair up your ass—and you and I both know it. He and his fucking …"

He stopped and peered around, making sure they were out of earshot of the others in the conference hall, "... spic whore have been strutting round Brazil like the fucking Peróns, kissing kids—ass and pussy too, by the sounds of it."

Pascalo grimaced at Savarge's foul language. "You think you know me, Owen, but you don't know me at all." Savarge gave him a contrary look that carried its own expletive. Pascalo acknowledged it and carried on regardless. "Anyway, Shar is a free agent now. BB won't stand in his way. Word is there's a wedding in the offing, so what's all the fuss? He wants to extend his last term. So what?"

"So *what?* So, he wants a fucking lot more than an extension—and you fucking know it. So don't gimme that innocent shit. The man's a goddamn enemy of the state! You know damn well what he wants. He wants—"

Pascalo had raised his hand to Savarge's face, blocking his words. "Stop right there. You are on the verge of speaking treason! People are listening. You realize treason still carries the death penalty?"

"Of course I fucking know—and I'd risk it... for America ... for the Republic!" He gave Pascalo a dismissive glare and turned away to Cusac. "Zack, you read the transcript yet?"

Cusac gave a troubled look. People were now staring at them. "Yes," he whispered. "But, for God's sake, keep your voice down."

"Well?" Savarge said, louder,

"You got access—read it yourself!"

"No, I ain't got *access,* that's why I'm fucking asking *you,* jackass! I've been denied! I'm only governor of DC—just a mere mortal. He's playing with us. The extension—did he fuckin' accept?"

People turned and stared at this outburst.

"Do you have to use such language?" asked Pascalo. "People are listening."

Savarge looked at him amazed.

"Such language?" He looked back to Cusac with puzzled eyes, "What the fuck have I said?"

Pascalo rolled his eyes. "God! Give me strength. And you're not Governor—you are Mayor."

"Governor/ Mayor, what the hell—to him I'm a goddamn plebe!"

The people stopped watching and turned back toward the screen.

Cusac gave the odd nod and smile, and then turned back to Savarge. "Extension? They offered him a complete extra term and—if he comes up with the goods—honorary presidency for life."

"Okay, okay. But, did he fucking accept?"

Cusac not hearing, continued, "God damn him… what's he holding out for?"

"What about the Nicaraguans?" asked Pascalo. "What did they say?"

Cusac shook his head, clearing the troublesome thought. "Nicaraguans? How the hell do I know? They spoke Nicaraguan—might as well been goddamn Greek. I just know he's got them eating out of his hand. He could do no wrong if he'd slept with every one of their goddamn daughters."

"Which he probably has," growled Savarge. "So, did he accept, for Christ's sake?"

"No, he didn't!" Cusac yelled. People were again staring at them. Cusac glared defiantly back at them and they looked away. He continued, his voice lowered. "His… gunsel, Vice President, made the gesture three times, so they say! We gotta watch Tunney—without Shar, he's a loose cannon."

Pascalo shook his head. "Tunney's no threat, he's powerless without Shar. If we take him too, it will seem like a coup d'état—that's not what we are about."

"Take him?" said Savarge. "What do you mean? Speak plainly. What are we about?"

Pascalo waved away this mounting, treacherous notion.

From across the hall, Shar entered with his entourage. Max greeted him cordially.

"J! Good trip?"

"Fine, just doodle dandy." He winked. "You feeling okay, Max? You look tired."

"Me? I'm fine, J. How about you? You get any sleep?"

Shar looked across to Savarge, and then turned back to Max with a mocking smile. "Yeah, I slept like a Senator."

Max gave a sour look. "Good for you."

"And you, Max? I like my team to sleep nights. Means they got a clear conscience." Shar patted Max's ample belly. "And I like them fat."

"Hey, man! I'm not *fat*—I work out."

Shar laughed. "A man who spends all his time in the gym, that's a sign of conceit: Got his fingers in someone else's business—or in somebody else's *wife*. Ha!" Shar laughed again and gave Max a searching stare. Max wondered if Shar was toying with him.

Shar looked across and studied Savarge. "Look at him, Max … Savarge. Looks like he don't sleep nights … he works out … got plugs in his hairline. He has that sleek, hungry look."

"Nah—he's kosher. He's apple pie."

"You noticed he looks taller of late? I heard the geek wears lifts."

Max smiled. "Beware of geeks wearing lifts."

"Hey—I do the sayings."

"Don't worry, J. Savarge is in the tent."

"Oh, yeah? Well, watch him anyways. I'm not looking for enemies, but if I were, he'd sure fit the bill. He has too big an opinion of himself for my comfort."

"Nah," grunted Max.

"You're too trusting, Maxwell. Take Savarge—you ever see him smile? He sneers … reminds me of Pooley. Never trust a skinny man who sneers. That's my new saying."

"Yeah? I'll remember that," said Max.

From the far side of the hall, Savarge looked resentfully at Shar. "What's the devious bastard up to? We've got to put a stop to this … stop it before it starts."

"I heard it started already," said Cusac as he focused his mind's-eye on some remote viewed image: Chad and Rena Menses, hands cuffed behind their backs, being led to the edge of the suburb, the city looming in the background. They are halted on a patch of shrubland, Rena looks to Chad, blows him a farewell kiss. A dozen shots split the night calm: the two fall.

Cusac shook away the troublesome image. "In Brazil, they are arresting all opposition. Hundreds—some say thousands. Killing everyone and anyone against the..." He stopped and looked furtively around the hall. "Not here ... it's too dangerous."

Savarge rolled his eyes, "Okay, okay, we'll meet. I'll be in touch with details—that includes you, Richard."

"No way ... include me out."

"You ain't fooling no one, General. I'll be in touch."

IV

In the oak-paneled study of the Jade Palace, Cloirina sat alone, writing. After a few moments, an elegantly dressed old man entered. Cloirina ignored him until she had finished her letter, then spoke without looking up.

"What is it, Uncle? Could you be quick? I'm busy."

"You have shamed this family," Walter Braganza said. "And you have shamed this—"

"How dare you!" Cloirina leapt to her feet. "You of all people. How dare you speak to me of shame?"

He looked away, knowing only too well what she was referring to. "That was a very long time ago."

"I have a very long memory."

"I am talking of Brazil. You have—"

"Don't you dare talk of Brazil! You who squandered our fortune in the casino. You who would have sold Brazil to the highest bidder."

"That is not true!"

"Shut up! Shut up!" she screamed into the old man's face. He backed away in shock. Cloirina clenched her fists, trying to contain her fury. "Now I am of age. I say what is or is not shame. I alone have put our family and our country back where it belongs."

"No, Cloirina—not alone. You will not sell yourself to that whoremonger. I forbid it."

"*Forbid?* Ha! You are nothing … a puppet. I let you play Presidente while I fight for our country's survival. You are there at my indulgence."

"I am—"

"Nothing—unless I say so." She saw weakness and defeat cloud the old man's eyes, and her anger subsided. "We *will* be great again, Uncle—and my child will inherit … that is all you need to know." The old man looked as if he would speak, but she continued. "And if you ever again criticize or attempt to chastise me, you will be out! I run this family!"

Her voice echoing around the room hid the sound of the door opening. Her teenage brother, Michael, had entered. "Not for long, sister," he said as he took up a supportive position beside the old man, "When I come of age, I will—"

"You will what?" Cloirina turned on him with spiteful anger, mocking his youthful attempt at bravado. "A lot can happen in four years, dearest Michael."

Michael smiled. He patted and pulled out the front of his shirt, mocking her pregnancy. "Yes. And a lot can happen in nine months, dearest Cloirina."

She suddenly leapt at him and slapped his face, knocking him back against the old man. "Nobody calls me dearest—except Janus Shar! And if you want to reach your twenty-first birthday, little brother, you'd better watch your tongue. You would do well to remember—

both of you—without Janus Shar, we are *all* lost. Now, leave me."

Michael, tears in his eyes, left the room, comforted by the old man. Cloirina returned to her writing, unconcerned.

In his small, private aircraft Cusac sat comfortably at the controls. Next to him, Owen Savarge sat nervously, his eyes tightly shut.

"So, what do you think of my new toy?" Cusac jauntily offered the controls, "Wanna take the stick? It's easy. Look." He gave the aircraft a couple of wing dips. "Just keep an inch of horizon above the instrument board. You wanna have a go?"

"No, I fucking don't!" Savarge gasped. "And don't fuck around—straighten the goddamn thing up! I hate flying at the best of times."

Cusac leveled the aircraft. He turned and smiled, indicating to the window with a nod. "Take a look down there."

Savarge opened his eyes momentarily and stole a nervous glance at the ominous clouds. "Yeah, yeah. Rough weather—so what?"

"So what? So there's rougher times ahead, Owen. We must have Pascalo's Presidential Guard. We need him with us."

"For what?"

"What the hell do you think, for what?"

"If we're going to eliminate him, say so. Revenge for Pooley, right?"

Cusac thought for a moment. "Yeah, I guess. Eliminate? Expand on that, Owen."

"Look, if Shar goes for purple, we go for scarlet—and fuck Pascalo, Presidential Guard or not. In or out?"

"You didn't hear me, Owen. Purple? Scarlet? Say what you mean. Kill? Assassinate? Speak plainly—extremely plainly. I want no misunderstanding."

"Kill! Murder! Assassinate! Take your fucking pick." Savarge closed his eyes again. "I'll do it with my own goddamn hands, if need be. Pooley was twice the man Shar is, but if he'd threatened the Republic, I'd have done the same."

Cusac leaned across and kissed Savarge full on the lips. Savarge did not repel him—he didn't even flinch or open his eyes.

Cusac sat back in his seat to study Savarge. "You did know that's how the Mafia seals a hit?"

"Yes, Zack, I did know that."

The two men sat in silence.

At length, Cusac smiled. "Anyways, Owen, do you think Pascalo will go for murder? I don't think so."

"He'll go for it," said Savarge with a devious grin. "I've made an appeal he can't refuse."

"An *appeal*?"

"Yeah—to his vanity. I sent a delegation to his home … with the dictates of the House."

"So? That's nothing to do with this."

"It is now. I appended a header and footer. Now it appears the whole Senate is for us, and endorses our cause. No way will he think to check it because the rest is sound. He don't have access anyway."

Cusac rubbed his brow in dread. "God have mercy. And if he does manage to check?"

Savarge's eyes sprang open. "Then to fuck with him! We lose nothing … status quo. But I'm betting he won't check because everybody knows Pascalo is an honorable man. It wouldn't occur to him that the document has been tampered with. Vanity … he'll do it for his people—his ego. As Oliver Cromwell said, *the dimensions of this mercy are above my thoughts."*

"Cromwell had the law on his side."

"Yeah, well we've got America on ours … right or wrong."

"When?"

"With Pascalo. Tomorrow."

"God, that soon! And without Pascalo?"

Savarge thought for a moment. "Still tomorrow. The king is dead! God save the republic, tomorrow! Now, let's stop flying up our own asses and go see if he's swallowed the bait."

The aircraft started its descent through the turbulent clouds. It was late evening and raining heavily when they landed. A limousine met them and Charles Ford, the fifty year-old governor of Mexico, sat in the back. Cusac and Savarge got in and flanked him. They nodded silent greetings as the limo sped off.

Richard Pascalo, clad only in swimming trunks, looked out over his magnificent estate. The warm, midsummer rainstorm danced a ramrod ballet across the surface of his swimming pool. After a few moments, an aide—black, sophisticated, and unashamedly gay—walked over with a large golf umbrella.

"What is it, Terence?" asked Pascalo as he was sheltered under the *Courvoisier*-emblazoned parasol. "Am I ordered in?"

"Sir, no, Sir," said Terence condescendingly, as if addressing an adolescent. "You still have time to play. However, a delegation from the Senate have called."

"Oh? And where are they?"

"Gone, Sir. The lady told them you were not to be disturbed. They left this, Sir." He handed an envelope on a tray. "Apparently no answer was expected."

"Thank you, Terence. Tell my wife that if anyone else calls, I am available. And tell her I'll be in soon."

"Yes, Sir. Would you like me to fix you some hot chocolate?"

"Chocolate? Have you ever known me to drink chocolate? Soldiers don't drink chocolate. Don't you know that?"

Terence smiled. *"Oh, you are a very poor soldier—a chocolate-cream soldier."*

"What! Who the hell said that?"

"Bernard Shaw—or was it Mark Twain? Someone with a beard—or was it a mustache? *You* should grow a mustache, Sir.

"Really? Did Mercedes tell you to ask?"

"Yes, Sir … she thought it might help you sleep—the chocolate, that is."

"Well, no thank you, Terence. Now leave me."

With a jerk of his hips, Terence nonchalantly spun around on his heels and walked away. When he was out of sight, Pascalo studied the document. As he skipped through the header and on through the footer, he started pacing, impervious to the rain that pitter-pattered onto the turning pages. He passed through a colonnade displaying marble busts of past Presidents and Foundling Fathers of the Republic. He spoke to them as addressing the living, pausing before Benjamin Franklin. "What would you have done, eh, Ben? Publish the Whaterly letters? No, don't answer … it may be a breach of honor—and I don't think that ploy would work this time. The people know already—and they don't care." He waved the delegation papers before the sightless eyes of the bust. "So it's left to just us few." He moved on to the shiny alabaster bust of Truman Pooley, and placed an arm lazily around the cloaked shoulders. "So, Pilgrim, between right or wrong, I choose America. Am I right, or am I right?" He paused as if waiting for a reply.

He turned now to the bust of Franklin D. Roosevelt. "So, you won the unprecedented third term. I wonder, had you survived, would we have granted you an extension, a fourth term?" He shook away the troublesome notion.

The rain was now running down his face. He gave his brow a cursory wipe with the papers and then confronted the bust of President MacArthur puffing eternally on his corncob pipe. "What do you say, Douglas? Would you return Janus Shar? I don't think so. I think you'd return the republic, nothing is more certain. Old soldiers never fade away; they stay and become President."

He shrugged and moved on to the bust of Washington. "Why me, George? No lies now—why me? Why can't they let me sleep with the rest of them?" He sighed, smiled sardonically, and moved on to the bust of Abraham Lincoln. Raising his hand, he spoke out in a mock oratory. "Fourscore and seven years ago, our fathers brought forth upon this continent a new nation, conceived in liberty. Wilkes Booth thought you had dictatoresque intentions. When any form of government becomes destructive, the people can exercise their constitutional right of amending it, or their revolutionary right to dismember. He took you at your word, Abe: *Sic semper tyrannis*."

Pascalo's wife, Mercedes, appeared at the open doors. She was graced with that rare beauty that time cannot spoil, but the lines about her elegant neck and the darkness of her eyes bore witness to its many attempts. She too, echoed Lincoln's words.

"Not bloody bullets, but peaceful ballots only are necessary," she whispered.

Pascalo turned to her, smiling. "Must I come in now—out of the rain?"

She returned a half smile. "Yes. Please."

"You know I love the rain. Makes everything so much cleaner. Just give me a few minutes. You go in … a few minutes."

Mercedes sighed deeply and returned to the house.

V

The limousine entered the long drive leading up to the Pascalo residence. In the rear, Savarge, Cusac, and Ford sat in leaden silence. The limo drove very slowly; they were in no hurry. The unspoken inductions—dangerous inductions—were tacitly understood. Through the rain-covered window, the three offered to the world a face of unyielding determination.

Pascalo climbed the steps to the top diving board and stood in the pouring rain, contemplating a swallow dive. He was lost in deep thought, arms swept back in readiness. After a few moments he lowered his arms to his sides and simply stepped off. He dropped, like Alice down her rabbit-hole, in a seemingly endless journey where images kaleidoscoped in his mind's eye. The pictures continued even as he penetrated the warm water. Through wide-open eyes and a swirl of bubbles, he saw subliminal flashes: police battling students; the communist witch-hunt trials; WW II atrocities; the assassination of Pooley, the empty cockpit, and then the explosion.

Now, with approaching hypoxia, the visions started to fade. Pascalo made an involuntary stroke, an instinctive attempt to surface, just as Terence entered the water fully clothed, in a convulsion of bubbles.

The two men burst to the surface, Pascalo, coughing, spluttering, and gasping. He had made the choice: life for himself, death for Shar.

Terence grabbed him, helped him to the edge of the pool, and then lifted him out and onto a seat. "Sir! You okay?"

"Sure … yeah," Pascalo coughed, sucking in deep breaths. "Okay now—thanks to you."

"You're getting too old for playing the Sub-Mariner," gasped Terence, trying to make light of the situation. "You sure you're okay?"

"Now I'm okay. Hot air and heavy rain, I love it. Go get some dry clothes—and *don't* tell Mercedes. And for God's sake, put on some music, will you, Terry? The sound of this rain is driving me crazy."

"Sure, I'll do that first. What'll it be … Viv, Chuck, or Claude?"

"Oh, Vivaldi. Tchaikovsky is too trivial for the mood I'm in. 'The Seasons.' I must be for all seasons, now." He thought for a moment. "No. On second thoughts, Debussy—it'll complement the rain."

"Good choice, Sir." Terence smiled. "I'll bring you a drink too, Sir."

"Terry, please don't call me Sir. It sounds, I don't know, so regal."

"Okay, General."

"Just for tonight, call me Richard, will you?"

Terence smiled again, "Sure … Rick. What's in a name?"

Savarge, Cusac, and Ford stood cheerlessly in the great portico of Pascalo's house. After a few moments, an aide greeted them and ushered them through to Mercedes in the great hall. She smiled as she formally addressed them, "Owen, Zachariah, and …" She hesitated, unable to recall the other name. "Sorry, I know your face, but I can't …"

"Ford, Mexico, governor of— Charley Ford, Ma'am, at your service."

"Oh, yes … my apologies. Isn't your brother—?" Again, she stopped, now fully remembering the troublesome details. "Oh, is he—?"

"Oh, yes Ma'am. My brother still rots in jail."

"Still?" She tried to show a degree of shock.

"Yes—at his majesty's pleasure, so to speak."

"You mean Janus Shar? I'm sorry."

"Yeah, so is my brother, Ma'am."

Embarrassed, Mercedes moved the conversation on. "So, what world-shattering business brings the three Magi out on a night like this?"

Savarge laughed. "There's no star to follow tonight, Ma'am. It's as black as hell out there. And it's far more serious than world shattering: a Masonic social needs organizing. It's a chore, but it's got to be done. Is he sleeping?"

"No," said Mercedes, wanting to believe the feeble lie. "He hardly sleeps at all lately. Terence will take you to him."

"Nice to see you, Mercedes," said Cusac. "More beautiful than ever."

"Why, Governor," she said, brightening slightly. "I do believe that was a compliment … someone's been working on you."

Cusac nodded graciously. "Must be the illustrious company I'm keeping." He gave a quick look to Savarge and Ford.

Mercedes smiled again and turned to make her exit. "Don't keep my husband too long, gentlemen. He seems to have the world on his shoulders these days." Then she was gone.

Terence entered in a dry, pristine uniform. He manufactured a disdainful smile and gave a dramatic bow. "This way, gentlemen."

Ford's smile was equally withering. "Lead on, boy."

Terence cocked his head. "Please don't call me 'boy,' Sir."

"Sure thing, kid. I didn't mean any slur."

"I know you didn't, Sir. I just like to bitch up a little … See what a poor lil' nigger-*boy* can get away with."

Cusac smiled to Savarge, both realizing Terence was toying with him.

Ford, sharing the joke, smiled. "Okay, cocksucker, lead on."

Terence, scoring his point, pirouetted daintily toward the garden. "That'll do nicely, Sir. Them as can, do, them as can't… walk this way, Mr. Ford … and the rest of you gentlemen."

Through the bottom of his martini glass, Richard Pascalo watched them approach. Now relaxed, he wore a dressing gown, which, in spite of it being soaked, gave him comfort. Its weight and the coolness would help keep his mind focused—he needed that.

Terence led them up to his table through the heavy rain. "Chuck, Zack, and Owen to see you, Rick—Voilà!" he announced with a majestic sweep of the hand as if presenting a meal. He then gave a sideways look toward Ford, smiled insincerely, and then arrogantly walked off.

Ford shrugged. "Seems a nice boy—kinda tall for this time of year—wouldn't you say, General?"

"Yes. I wouldn't say."

"Let's go inside, Richard," said Ford, turning up his coat collar. "We're getting soaked."

"No, it's safer here, Charlie." Pascalo gave a wicked smile. "You know what spies say—do your plotting near running water—it interferes with the wire. Any of you people wearing wires?" Ford spluttered a protest. Pascalo raised his hand. "A joke! Maybe my last."

"God, let's hope so," said Ford, wryly. "So, you seen the delegation papers?"

"These?" Pascalo picked up the bunch of soggy papers. "Yes, I did. They've all but named him *enemy of the state* ... such an ancient concept. So, when?"

"When?" Savarge chipped in, "When what? Speak plainly, General."

"When do we kill this enemy of the state? Plain enough?"

"Tomorrow," Savarge answered abruptly, barely containing his shock at Pascalo's directness. "It's got to be tomorrow—before he accepts; before the precedent is set."

"How?"

"The American way," said Cusac. "Head shot … no mistakes … three shots, three snipers."

"No. Not that." Pascalo raised the papers, waved them as if to wave away the idea. "For God's sake. Not that. We must do it, and everybody must see. We don't want another conspiracy nightmare … we must do it openly and without rancor or malice."

"How?" said Cusac.

Pascalo shrugged. "The Italian way, up close and personal—the blade."

"Jesus wept!" gasped Savarge, wiping the rain from his face, "Jesus fucking wept."

"Yes," said Pascalo, "and I believe he will again, for all of us."

"Which of us will do it, General?" Cusac glanced conspiratorially at Savarge, and then to Ford.

"All! We all do it … each one of us makes his own cut."

Cusac shuddered. "Okay, General. I'm for that. Let's all swear an oath."

"No!" Pascalo said. "No swearing of oaths. This is not conspiracy; this is purely and simply unavoidable. The Senate say he threatens the very Republic; we take them at their word, their sanction. We stab him to death in full view of the Senate. Tomorrow."

The four men were silent. The only sound was the faint strains of music under the foreboding patter of rain.

Savarge was the first to react. "That is if he goes to the Senate tomorrow."

"What do you mean?" said Cusac. "Why wouldn't he go?

Savarge thought for a moment, "Well, he don't always. With the current situation, his people don't like him to be too predictable."

"His people?" For the first time, Pascalo raised his voice. *"I'm* his people—the Presidential Guard. I'm going to reassign his security. He'll be there tomorrow. I have it on the best authority ... I feel it in my bones."

"I'll be there on breakfast call tomorrow," growled Cusac. "I'll make damn sure he comes."

Savarge shrugged and expelled the breath he'd unwittingly been holding. "Yeah, that's good ... we all travel with him to the Capitol, right? Right?"

Ford hesitated a moment, then nodded. "Okay, no other business ... the simpler, the better. We do it as he enters the Senate."

Pascalo remained silent, his eyes spoke the word he could not make his mouth utter. Without further comment, Savarge, Cusac, and Ford walked back into the house, leaving Pascalo to the rain and Debussy.

Mercedes received them in the great hall with a smile. "So, gentlemen, have you put the world to rights ... your social?" She again smiled as she led them through to the main door to where Terence waited. She looked at Savarge, waiting for his answer.

"Oh ... I think so, Ma'am," he said, searching for words, and then turned to Ford. "Chuck? What do you say?"

Ford responded with a withering, tooth-clenched leer, damning Savarge for putting him on the spot. He turned to Mercedes, managing to lighten the smile.

"Ask us this time tomorrow, Ma'am. And please, try to make the general get some sleep, will you? Big day tomorrow … Mid-Term. Goodnight, Mercedes."

She nodded graciously and made her exit, leaving Terence to lead them to the door. The three men reluctantly stepped outside, bracing themselves against the rain. Terence escorted them under the huge golf umbrella to their waiting limousine. Bowing in mock humility, he closed the door behind them and then returned to the house. Shaking the rain from the umbrella, he hurried back inside to find Mercedes waiting.

She sighed and gave him a sad smile. "You can leave, too, Terry. See you in the morning."

"Ma'am, you feeling okay?" He could feel her unhappiness, but there was little he could do or say—other than offer his cheery, girl-to-girl camaraderie. "Would you like me to make you some hot chocolate? And how about some of your favorite cookies to dunk? You deserve a treat after them horrid, horrid … men."

"No, I feel fine, really. Goodnight, Terry."

Terence theatrically kissed the back of his hand, and gently blew it to her. "Good night, Madam. Sleep tight."

She smiled again—this time a happier one—and then walked off in the direction of the garden.

Richard Pascalo was finishing his second martini as Mercedes joined him. The delegation papers, half read, made a puddle on the table in front of him. She looked down at him for a few seconds. He could feel her questions burning into his brain.

"Why?" she asked, raising the last part of the single syllable dramatically.

"Why what?" he said, trying to sound puzzled.

"Oh, just … why? Why up so late? Why can't you sleep? Why do three dignitaries call in the middle of the night—in a storm? Just … why?"

He shook his head and smiled. "It's nothing, dear. I'll come to bed."

"Why?" The same irritating diphthong. "You won't sleep … you won't make love to me … Why?"

"I try not to worry you, because—"

"Because of these?" She turned on him angrily, displaying her scarred wrists. "It was this that drove me to do it—this not knowing. It's not fair, Richard, I'm born to this. My father supported Pooley right to the bitter end. He confided in my mother—they were a team. You're robbing me of my birthright, for God's sake."

Pascalo took her scarred wrists, holding them tenderly. "Honey, there's nothing to tell—just that I love you, I've always loved you, and I always will love you. Now, come to bed."

Mercedes sighed—not in frustration, but in defeat. "Will you sleep?" she asked, already knowing the answer.

"No!" He let go of her wrists and smiled playfully. "We have some unfinished business first… then we'll *both* sleep." She returned his smile.

He put his arm around her waist and they walked into the house.

VI

Betty Shar lay sleeping in her sumptuous bed, alone. The approaching dawn saw the raindrops of the previous night's storm blow away from the window in the light breeze. It was well past the witching hour, but for BB, the demons of nightmare had dallied. Her eyes moved erratically under the lids as she entered troubled dream-sleep. In total silence, she saw the prelude to Pooley's fatal flight to Brazil: Him waving to the cheering crowds at Sonora airfield—the flight over the Brazilian mountains—the single parachute falling away from the aircraft—then, finally, the crash. She sat up, seemingly awake, but there at the end of the bed, drenched in blood, stood Truman Pooley. Even though his head was half-smashed, he was smiling. In his extended hand was an ornate baton—a silver eagle with spread wings at its crest. He was offering it to Janus, who now stood beside him. But as Shar reached to take it, Pooley struck out, hitting him again and again. Over and over, the eagle's wings smashed his face and head, smashing, banging, banging, banging. Betty screamed, but it was the mute scream of nightmare. Banging, banging. She screamed again; somewhere in this netherworld of dream she found her voice. "Naaaaa! Noooo, no! No! Noooo!"

A knocking on the adjoining door replaced the banging. The dream within a dream truly ended as Shar burst into the room and grabbed her.

"Betty! Dear God, Baby. Hey, it's okay … just a bad dream."

"Oh, it was horrible. Horrible!"

"It's okay now, I'm here." Shar cradled her convulsing body. "Hush, Baby, hush. You shouldn't sleep alone. We should—"

"We should what?" Betty abruptly stopped crying and was now fully awake. She stared blankly into her husband's face. "I don't think so, do you? I just agreed to come back to the White House until you win your extension, no more. Nothing has changed—you haven't changed—you just need me here."

Shar offered a magnificent rendering of deep hurt. She'd seen it before. "That's just not true, Betty," he said, his eyes flooding with forced tears. "What else can I say? It didn't mean anything—it was just business. I was lonely, all the clichés wrapped up in one. I'm sorry."

"Sorry—it's so easy to say, isn't it?"

"Yes, easy to say … not so easy to mean. But I do, and I'll be sorry for the rest of my life. And I'll say sorry every day of my life until you believe me."

Betty turned her eyes away. "There's been someone else, J. I thought you were gone for good this time. I just felt you ought to know. I hate deceit."

"I guessed as much." His wounded look seemed to deepen. "No, don't tell me who it was. It must be someone I know; we are a very insular group. You're not still …? Is it over?"

"Is it ever over?" She was close to tears. "That part of it is. Now it's just the heartache."

Shar put his hands to his head in anguish. "Jesus, I'm sorry, Betty."

"Hey!" She forced a smile. "You already said today's sorry—tell me again tomorrow."

Shar lowered his crocodile eyes. Betty smiled again as she took his hand, "Please don't go, Janus." He raised his head, returned the smile, and then reached for her.

Betty pulled away. "No, not that."

"What, then? Anything?"

"I mean don't go to the Senate today. Stay home with me. I … I dreamed Pooley killed you; beat you to death with a silver baton. Janus, don't go to the Senate today. Not today."

"I have to go." There was a note of submission in his voice. "It's Mid-term … it's my duty, Baby. I have to."

The avenue outside Blue Haven was already lined with crowds, many of whom had been there all night. This State-of-the-Nation debate was something special; somehow, the people knew of The Americas deal and Shar's need for an extra term to clinch it. It was the best, worst kept secret of the decade. Everybody felt there was something in it for them.

BB came from her shower and pulled on her robe. She hesitated as she pondered her horrific dream, then shook away the troublesome images and walked into the bedroom. Shar was sitting on the bed, fully clothed. "Well?" she asked. She didn't smile; she didn't even look at him as she spoke. "Are you going?"

"Yes, as I said. You know I have to."

"You don't have to."

"I do. I need this extra term."

"The people don't want this, J. The latest opinion poll clearly shows that."

Shar stood up. He never liked looking up when he was arguing; somehow it made him feel vulnerable.

"You can't rely on opinion polls," he said as he paced. "They show you what the hell you want them to show. The people have no heart. Money, money, money … it is what they want. And if I offer it, they'll take it, that you can rely on. They do want this, and—" A knock on the door cut him short. Shar composed himself. "Yes? It's okay, come in."

A female aide entered. "Sir, Ma'am, they're here, and Governor Cusac. I've shown them into the summer suite. Will you be taking breakfast?"

"None for me, Rose," said Betty, now totally composed. "Just tea, here."

Shar thought a moment. "None for me, either. Just coffee—we'll take it here. Give us half an hour and then we'll join them. Thank you."

Security forces shepherded the gathering crowds back from the avenue approaching the Senate. A fly-by was expected. A squadron of Paragon VTJs—vertical take-off jets—would hover above the President's entourage as it made its triumphal way.

It was mid-morning as Janus Shar and BB made their entrance into the crowded breakfast room to a chorus of hellos and good mornings. Most of the diners had finished eating, and were standing around in groups.

Shar joined the largest. "Sorry, everybody," he said, offering a face of regret, "but it seems I shall not be attending today."

There were gasps of disappointment.

BB looked up at Shar, happily surprised. "You won't regret it, J."

Cusac moved close to Shar, took his arm, and led him a little way away. "God sakes, Janus," he whispered. "Why? What the hell do I tell the Senate?"

"Tell them I will not be there today. Tell them I'm needed at home." He smiled at BB and then turned back to Cusac. "Goddamn it, man, think of something. That's what you're here for, isn't it?"

Lost for words, Cusac stared back at him. Shar took his arm and moved him farther from BB's earshot. "Sorry, Zack, but BB isn't well. She experienced a bad dream. She needs me here. This Brazilian thing has taken its toll."

"Yeah, but—"

"Look, if she drops me now, I'm finished. I've got to toe the line on this one—you know what's at stake. Tell them anything. Stall! Anyways, just because I'm President don't mean I don't get a private life."

Cusac shrugged. "Okay, I'll tell them. Just that today is so important: Mid-term, and all. There's a flyover of jets expected. The whole Senate is about to offer the presidency ... for life! Both sides."

"Both?" gasped Shar.

"Yes, both—even the remnant coalition parties. Not a single veto. And they're all expecting you to accept. I'll tell them ... I don't know, BB had a bad dream, I guess..." He turned away, making to walk off. "Jesus!"

Shar shrugged toward BB, and then turned back to Cusac. "Okay, okay, I'll come. And if BB kicks me out again, I'll be coming home with you, Zack."

Cusac closed his eyes in relief. Shar smiled to a stony-faced BB and then turned back to Cusac. "I can't do no right." Cusac reciprocated with a Judas smile of sympathy.

Pascalo and Savarge now joined them. Pascalo forced a smile. "BB, Mr. President, nice morning ... after the storm."

"Richard. Why so formal?"

"Oh ... it's a formal kind of day."

"Really?" Shar gave him a quizzical look. "And where is my Vice President on this formal kind of day? I'll travel with Max."

"We'll travel in the middle car," said Pascalo, ignoring the question. "You, Owen, Zack, and myself."

Shar looked annoyed. "No. That won't do—I want Max to travel with us."

"Max is late, as usual." Pascalo hated lying, but it wasn't a total lie. Max was, indeed, late. "Anyway, we want him in the next car ... keep them guessing. Right hand don't need to know what the left foot is doing."

Pascalo resolved to test Shar's intentions one final time. "So, J, do I get a garter out of this?"

Shar was taken aback and slightly embarrassed. He studied Pascalo; he had not expected him to condone. "Nah, Richard, it wouldn't suit you; you haven't got the knees for a garter. How about a coronet?"

"I won't hold you to that, Mr. President," said Pascalo; his remaining doubts draining away to total commitment.

VII

Both sides of Grand Avenue were filled with crowds, cheering and waving star-spangled banners. The Paragon VTJs had arrived on cue and were now hovering, one every hundred yards, over Shar and his entourage as the six black limousines made their way toward the great marble-faced building. Once inside the House, the Presidential Guard encircled Shar, who now took the opportunity to study his speech notes, experimenting with various hand gestures and expressions. Pascalo stood staring, waiting for the moment.

When Max Tunney entered, he was immediately surrounded by a group of Presidential Guards barring his way. He pushed roughly through them and approached Shar.

"Sorry I couldn't make breakfast call this morning, J. My usual security call didn't happen. Instead I get the goddamn Presidential Guard! What's wrong with them guys? They tried to stop me getting through!"

"You shouldn't live alone, Maxwell. You need a wife of your own."

Max gave him a searching look. "So *you* say. What the hell's going on, Janus?"

Shar shook his head despondently. "God alone knows, Max. They think we're getting complacent."

"Well, I wish they'd let me, the Vice President, know."

"That, Max, is the whole point! You're not supposed to know. I don't even know."

"I don't like this." Max shook his head. "This is Pascalo's play."

Shar smiled. "Pascalo is a confident man, and you know what I always say…"

"'What you get is what you see' or something like that?"

"No, I don't say that any more, not since Brazil. If I'm to get in the *Book of Quotations*, it won't be with that. My new saying is, 'Never argue with a confident man.'"

Max smiled. "Oh? I thought it was 'Never trust a skinny man who sneers.' Anyways, how you feeling? You know you don't look too good. You get any sleep?"

Shar laughed out loud. "To hell with you. I feel fine. You should always make breakfast call, Max. People speak the truth over breakfast; it's over dinner that they lie."

"Sorry. Was that another new saying?"

Shar studied his Vice President. "You're looking thin, Max—and was that a sneer?"

Max gave a grudging smile. "Arrr … nuts! Look, I'm going to find Marshall. I'm going to sort this out."

As Max walked off, a woman edged up to Shar. Deloris Marshall: head of ISS—Internal Senate Security. She was attractive to the extreme, but possessed that hard, purposely unfeminine, android-like persona that her eminent post demanded.

"I waited until Tunney had gone, Sir," she said from the corner of her mouth. "I know that schmuck is looking for me."

"Now, now, Deloris. That's no way to speak about my Vice President."

"I know he's going to break my balls over this, Sir."

"A Bee-Scout must be brave, Deloris."

The masculine facade momentarily lifted and she afforded herself a smile. "*Hippity-Hoppity Goes to Town,* right Sir? My favorite movie."

"That's right, Deloris … be brave."

The smile vanished. "Sir, we want you to wear this."

"The hell is that?"

"It's just a lightweight flack shirt, Sir."

"Looks like a goddamn corset. Nah, I never wear that stuff. Didn't do Pooley one hell of a lot of good."

"But Sir, it's not bulky … just like a vest. It's covered with the same material as your suit."

"How the—"

"We had three made, Sir. We didn't know what suit you'd be wearing."

"Oh! So, I'm Billy Three-Suits, eh?"

"It doesn't weigh much, Sir … it bends with your body … made of some kind of magic-putty."

"Take it away, Deloris, and don't fuss me. There's a good girl."

Cusac joined them. "Hey, what's this, Marshall? You take your instruction from Pascalo—the President don't want it, he don't want it."

"Ms. Marshall, to you, Governor. And what the hell's going on? Why the break in protocol?"

Cusac gave Shar a clandestine look. Shar turned away, slightly amused. Cusac looked back at Deloris. "Well, *Ms* Marshall, it's Mid-term, and—"

"So what?"

"So what? If you give me a chance to explain—it's all change. You guys are getting sloppy, Vice President's orders. You got a problem, take it up with him. He's out there in the portico—I saw him just a moment ago. And, hey! If you're gonna bitch, do it now. Don't bust his balls in front of the cameras, take him into the annexe."

"Go to hell! What do you take me for, your goddamn gofer, for Christ sakes?" She turned to Shar and gave an apologetic smile. "Sorry, Sir."

Cusac watched her walk away. "Ohwee!"

Shar shrugged and shook his head.

Mercedes sleepily slid an arm into the empty space next to her. The absence of her husband woke her abruptly. She looked about, half expecting him to appear from the bathroom. He didn't.

Now fully awake, she pulled the cord beside her bed. After a few moments, Terence entered.

"Ma'am?"

"Terry, where's my husband?"

He looked puzzled, "Why, he's gone, Ma'am, to the Senate. Mid-term."

"But I was to accompany him." She raised her voice slightly. "What time is it?"

"It's ten, Ma'am… almost ten."

She tried to think. "Terry, you have to find him. You must go. Go now, and find him. Insist he comes back with you."

"But, Ma'am, that's not possible. It's the Senate! No one's allowed in."

Mercedes was desperate. She could feel the blood pulsing in her temples. "You must! Tell someone to get a message to him. Tell him anything! Lie. Say I've taken an overdose … anything!"

Terence stood ashen-faced. Now he was scared. Whatever it was that his mistress feared now touched him. "Yes, Ma'am… anything, anything!" He began to panic. "But … but, Ma'am," he mumbled as he switched on the TV, "it's already started!"

"You must, Terry. You must!"

"I'll go straight away, Ma'am. But the crowds … I'll just go."

As he hurried from the room, the TV came to life. Live coverage showed the assembled Senate waiting for the doors to open. Mercedes watched in dread.

For the first time in years, Shar was nervous. It was midday as he made ready to enter. His speech was well rehearsed and he'd been assured there would be no surprises. Shar knew what he needed, the Senate knew what he needed, and the people knew what he needed to broker the greatest prize since the annexation of Canada. The Americas had been all but sanctioned. Yes, there was opposition—strong opposition—but money and ambition ruled the day. He had put his own fortune, his family's fortune, and indeed his entire conglomerate stocks and holdings on the line. Risking all these monies could cost him dearly if he failed—even his life. Could he do all this and not get a … ? He dared not think or say the word aloud. But he, America—North and South—and the whole world had heard the word crystal clear.

As his nerve started to waver, the doors mercifully opened. Shar took a deep breath and then strode in ahead of his aides. As he entered, a cheer went up.

Over the noise, a voice called out. "You beware them Mid-term blues, Mr. President."

Shar turned toward the poignant voice, smiling as he remembered where he'd first heard those words. "Hey! Who is that? I heard that in Brazil. Were you in Brazil?"

The voice called out again. "Beware them Mid-term blues."

Shar gave a cursory wave as he walked on past the voice. "Mid-term is passed—nevertheless I will. I will."

A few feet away, Charles Ford stood rigid, just inside the portico. His face was completely devoid of color, and his feet felt like lead. As Shar moved toward the lectern, it was with extreme effort that Ford stepped forward, barring his way. "Mr. President," he said dryly, sucking his tongue for moisture. "Before you start. I have a petition. Half the Senate has signed it. My brother, he is still in jail. He—"

"What's this?" Shar stopped, angry at the interruption. "Goddamn, you want me to spring your brother, is that it? Like some connected hoodlum?"

Ford took a paper from his pocket and thrust it at Shar. "Half the Senate has signed, Mr. President. You must reconsider."

As Ford spoke, two groups of Presidential Guard, one from either side, converged, cutting off Shar from his aides. Unaware, Shar continued.

"*I* must reconsider? What the hell do you think this is? Your brother was tried … tried and convicted. Did the grand jury beg for mercy? No. Your brother wanted one of my stars!"

"He did nothing unconstitutional." Ford again brandished the partition. "Mexico was never his aspiration, he was railroaded … by someone else's aspirations!"

Shar pushed the paper away. "That's not what the grand jury said. And even if I wanted to, no way could I intervene. In all its history, America has never lost a star. They're set in the flag like the stars in the sky. You and your scurrilous brother would find it easier to take one of those."

Mercedes, still in nightclothes, sat on her bed staring into the TV screen that was showing live coverage of Shar's approach to the Senate. She registered nothing of these images flickering in front of her eyes—just those conjured in her mind: the demise of Truman Pooley.

First, his brother Silus in the company of a notorious drug baron, shot dead in a seedy, male bordello in Argentina. Then, through tear-flooded eyes, she saw the last flight of Truman Pooley, more lifelike than the pictures on the TV. At his departure, he, standing at the aircraft door, pausing to wave. She, together with other dignitaries, bidding him farewell. Then the imagined crash, Pooley screaming as the aircraft plummeted.

Four miles across the city, Betty Shar sat in front of her wall-sized TV monitor. The same broadcast was playing.

Shar gave a dismissive look to Ford, and then made to move forward. A shake of the head from Pascalo and the circle of guards remained closed. Shar seemed puzzled, but accepted it as a precautionary stratagem. Pascalo now approached. A nod to the guards and the circle opened, allowing him access to Shar and Ford.

"God's sake, Janus!" Pascalo's voice boomed, echoing around the cavernous marble vestibule. "Show some pity … the man is begging!"

Shar was taken aback. This was not like Pascalo—nor was it his place to involve himself in politics. "What, Richard, you're in on this charade too?"

"Just in this, Janus. Please… I'm sorry!"

"Dear God, man. You're the one who's begging!"

Savarge and Cusac stepped into the circle. Another nod from Pascalo and the ring closed, leaving Shar surrounded. There was a moment of clarity. Shar knew in that instant that the unthinkable was about to happen. He looked at them, one to the other, studying each face for a trace of pity, but it seemed an age of silence. Then, as if in answer to some unspoken command, Savage pulled his ice pick from his jacket and hurled forward. "He goes!" he yelled as he stabbed Shar under the right armpit, forcing the weapon up into his body. "He goes!"

Shar staggered and took a step forward, his eyes begging the question: 'Why?' as Cusac lunged from behind.

Ford stabbed out with his ice pick, plunging it into Shar's throat. He seemed not to react to this third thrust; he just stared into Ford's eyes, searching. However, no answer was to be found here. He stumbled drunkenly around the enclosed circle until he found Pascalo. Surely the answer would be here? Pascalo closed his eyes and, expelling a single tear, stabbed blindly, the final blow into Shar's chest. Shocked and bloodied, Shar slipped to the floor, close to death. His eyes had already lost their humanity; they had the look of an animal at the threshold of the slaughterhouse. After a fleeting moment, they closed.

VIII

Terence had arrived just moments after Shar's demise. In spite of his connection with General Pascalo, he had not been allowed access. On the contrary, he had, with countless others, been placed under cursory arrest. He could not even contact Mercedes to give her the small amount of information he had gleaned—much good it would have done.

Mercedes sat motionless in front of the TV, eyes staring, but seeing nothing—neither on the screen nor in her visions. Like Shar, she too was all but dead—her wrists slit with her letter-opener, weeping the remnants of her life's blood into a widening pool at her feet.

The Presidential Guard's rifles tightly encircled the group. More guards were positioned at every exit, holding back the enraged crowd. Inside the circle, the conspirators stood around the bloody body of their President. Savarge, still clutching the gory ice pick, gazed helplessly at Pascalo. He looked as if he was about to vomit. Pascalo pried the weapon from his hand, dropping it to the floor. He shook Savarge, attempting to exorcise the trauma of the last few moments.

"It's okay, Owen," he said gently. "Owen, it's done! Think, man." Savarge only partly heard, and then a new shock as Pascalo slapped him hard across his face. "Think, man, think! Now is the difficult part. My men have the TV station … we go to air in one hour. One hour, we go public! Owen, are you listening?"

"Yes … yes! Jesus Christ!" The slap had jolted him back to cold reality, "We really did it?"

"Affirmative. The king is dead—God save the Republic. Now what you do is hold on, Owen. You must stay calm—we must all stay calm." Pascalo directed his words to Cusac and Ford. "We must move on."

"Jesus Christ in heaven." Ford mumbled into his blood-spattered hand. "We did it."

Pascalo turned from him. He spoke sharply to the captain of the guard. "Stay calm, soldier. Let those medics through."

The circle of guards parted, allowing through two visibly shocked medics. One, in forlorn hope, carried plasma. Before the circle closed, Deloris Marshall pushed her way in, "I'm with the medics, back off!" She spat her words at a young soldier. The guard balked, but Pascalo nodded permission. As she entered, she stopped abruptly at the blood pool, almost stepping into it. She righted herself and then stared in disbelief at Shar's ruptured corpse, brutally ripped, slashed, and torn. After a moment, she managed to turn away. She focused an incredulous, icy stare on Pascalo. "You? You did this?"

Pascalo stared back, and then averted his eyes past her, as if searching the crowd. "Where's Tunney, Deloris?"

She concentrated her stare, making it unavoidable. "You did this!" Her voice neared hysteria.

"Marshall, there isn't time," said Pascalo. "Freedom and liberty, remember? America is the longest surviving republic in the world. Where is Tunney?"

"Gone!" Marshall yelled. "Gone with the others!" Her gaze was drawn back to the body, now an island in a widening scarlet ocean. "You did this?" she screamed. "You did this … fucking murder?"

Pascalo was silent. Savarge, regaining his resolve, stepped up to Deloris. "Yes! We did this murder, and yes, we will have to answer for it. But there are things to be done first."

She turned away, back to Pascalo. "Done?"

"Yes. You must keep order until we go on air … then we'll know. There's no other way now." She attempted to cut in, but Pascalo continued over her. "We couldn't have a monarchy. In time, people will see—will understand. God's death, Deloris, America couldn't have a king!"

Deloris was shocked into silence. Pascalo turned to the captain of the guard. "Escort Ms. Marshall out. The medics, too." Then a final word to Deloris as the guard led them away. "Find Tunney. Tell him he is safe and that I want to talk. He has my word of honor."

Again, she attempted to speak, but Pascalo cut her off. "Deloris, we couldn't have a king."

Ford moved off with the guard. "I'll go with her to make sure. We need to hear from Tunney ... desperately."

More Presidential Guardsmen now cleared the hall. People were weeping openly, arguing, and some actually fighting to get close to the corpse. A sudden shriek of static as the speaker system boomed:

"To all free Americans ... a TV press conference will commence in one hour. To all free Americans ..." The message repeated over and over until the hall was eventually cleared. The conspirators stood alone, looking down on Shar's body. It lay askew, as it had fallen, one hand raised, hiding his eyes, as if ashamed to let his bloody face be seen. Raised up behind the corpse was a heroic posed painting of President Truman Pooley.

Pascalo gave an ironic sigh. "So the Brothers Grim got their revenge."

Cusac shrugged. "I guess."

Ford hurried back to rejoin the circle. "Open up!" The guard allowed him to pass. "There's a messenger," he gasped to Pascalo, catching his breath, "from Tunney! He wants to talk!" Ford immediately beckoned the messenger to approach.

The aide stood to attention before Pascalo, and swallowed nervously. "General, Maxwell Tunney agrees to meet—immediately if possible. He's waiting outside. He wants assurances from you all. He asked me to tell you he believes you all to be honorable men." The aide paused, compelled to look at Shar's body.

"Is that all?" said Pascalo. "Is there more?"

The aide broke from his trance. "Yes, there is more. He... he says he is with you, now that President Shar is ..." He stopped again, and again was compelled to look at the body of his President. He continued, eyes wide, still in disbelief, "Now that Shar is ... dead. But he demands an explanation. He wants to help you through this hazardous time. What do I tell him?"

"Tell him he can come and leave at will ..." Pascalo looked around to include his coconspirators. To a man, they dutifully nodded their consent, "...whatever the outcome of our discussions."

"Yes, Sir... General." The aide spoke mechanically, unable to tear his gaze from the gruesome remains at his feet. Pascalo nodded to the captain of the guard. The guard took the mesmerized man and led him out of the circle. Cusac attempted to speak. Pascalo waved away the unspoken notion, reassuring him. "Don't worry, Zack. Tunney will offer no threat."

Ford put his hand to his mouth again, as if to prevent some weakness he might utter.

Savarge sighed deeply. "I wish I had your confidence, Richard."

Pascalo looked at Savarge, then down at Shar's body. "Never argue with a confident man." He looked toward the corpse. "Sorry, Janus, I ... ah! —Here comes Tunney."

The ring of guards opened to let Max through. Pascalo greeted him with a nod. "Tunney."

Max walked past Pascalo and knelt in the blood by Shar's body. He haplessly felt the bloody neck for a pulse. "Christ, you've cut him to pieces!" After a moment, he stood up and looked Pascalo in the eye. "Why?"

"Max," Pascalo said softly but with menace. "You know why."

Max pinched his eyes, forcing the tears back across his temple. "Even his enemies wouldn't have done this. But you—you were his friend!"

"Yes, yes, I was his friend—and yours, too. Whatever way you turn, Maxwell, you are free to walk out. But first I ask you … think!"

"Okay, I've thought. Now, how the hell was he so dangerous as to warrant this?"

"Christ, Max, you know what he wanted!"

"He wanted the chance for an extra term."

"We'd have given him that extra term; we'd even given life presidency. Goddamn it, he wanted it hereditary … a monarchy."

"That's not so," said Max, choosing his words carefully. "That was something dreamed up by Cloirina Braganza. She thought Janus was going to marry her."

"Max, it's done. I go on air in an hour—live in front of the Senate—and broadcast to the whole country. The entire nation will be watching. Everything will be explained. We have the Constitution on our side. Shar was deemed an enemy of the state. Right or wrong, I chose America. America is the victor in this."

"That's Pooley talking," said Max with contempt.

"It's done, Max!"

Max thought for a moment. "You'll let me speak? To give eulogium?"

Pascalo looked to Savarge, whose frowning eyes said a definite no. Pascalo turned back to Max. "Yes," he said bluntly.

Savarge rolled his eyes in disbelief. Taking Pascalo by the arm, he walked him away from Max. "What the hell did you say yes for? The people love him, for Christ sakes. He'll turn them."

"Don't worry," said Pascalo, "I'll have his word. I'll speak first. They'll see there was no other way—there *was* no other way. If there had been, we'd have taken it. What can he say to that now? You okay?"

"I guess," said Savarge.

"Right. You and Owen are radio and overseas, I'm live TV... and you, Charlie, you handle the immediate press. We want everybody to hear at the same time ... no speculation."

Savarge scowled. "I still don't like the Tunney angle."

"It's done." Pascalo's tone put an end to further comment. Savarge, Ford, and Cusac left with a guard escort.

Pascalo moved back to Max. "So, Maxwell, we have control of the TV stations. You can speak, but you don't damn us. Just tell them of all the good of the man. You can add that although you're not one of us, you speak with our sanction. Name us, but don't blame us. Agreed?"

"Agreed." Max had to force the word out. "Now I need a minute with him alone. Will you grant me that?"

Pascalo nodded, and then walked away. Max knelt by the body, alone except for the inert ring of guards.

"J, I'm sorry," he said, choking back the tears. "I'm sorry if I seem too lenient with these butchers. God, look at you … Why?" He stood up and hurled his words to the glass-domed ceiling. "I swear to every American—and to God Almighty—I will smash each damn, murdering one of them." The circle of guards turned on him. There was a loud metallic clatter as their weapons simultaneously cocked.

Max confronted the young captain. "You up for this, Son—this fucking treason? Are you prepared to hang with the rest? This is insurrection—goddamn civil war!"

The officer shrank back. "Sir … I … I can't let you pass."

Max grabbed the barrel of the captain's weapon, forcing it away from his face. "Get the hell out of my way, you fucking traitor!" He pushed past the terrified soldier and strode off.

IX

In the Senate House quadrangle, Max waited by the helipad. It was just minutes until his helicopter circled and landed in a cloud of dust and freshly mown grass. The pilot had no time to cut the engine as Max took the full force of the rotors and climbed aboard. He brushed himself off, sat down and belted up.

An aide shouted over the engine noise as he closed the door. "Sir! I'm personal aide to Wesley Shar. He's on his way in … flying from Alaska at his uncle's invitation. He doesn't know yet. Someone … I have to speak to him."

Max gave a gasp of realization. "Wes! Poor kid. I'd forgotten about him. You have to tell him immediately."

The aide looked as if he was about to throw up. "Yes, Sir. I suppose it has to be me. But how … what—"

"Tell him he's in great danger here. Tell him he must divert to Vancouver Island—there's a naval base, my home territory … Admiral Keating. I'll arrange it

— thank God for my navy. Tell him … tell him to turn on the TV."

"But Sir … I … I … he loved Shar like a father. I can't … The President, it's so …"

"Okay, I'll do it. Get him on line and I'll speak to him on the way to the TV station, then I'll speak to Keating."

The helicopter took off as the aide made the call. He handed Max a helmet with radio link.

Max fiddled with the projecting microphone. "Wesley? Wes, it's Max Tunney. I got to tell…" He sighed with relief. "Okay, you know already. I'm so sorry, Wes. I know how much he meant to you. He was a great man, and them murdering bastards are gonna pay … but not yet."

In his private jet, Wesley Shar, an effeminate young man of nineteen, was openly weeping into the telephone. "I'm coming home, Uncle Max. I—"

"No!" Max shouted. "You have to wait. Divert to Vancouver Island. I'll arrange things."

"I have to see his body first, Uncle Max."

"No, no! It's an order … I am acting President. I forbid it. It's too dangerous."

"I must, Uncle Max. I must!"

Max thought for a moment. It was his decision, but the boy had that right. "Okay, but it's dangerous. You come in, pay your respects, then get the hell out. They've got the Presidential Guard and the army, but I got my navy. Watch the TV. If things look bad, go to Brazil … Cloirina Braganza … I'll set that up too."

"But, Uncle—"

"Wes, there's no time. I'm sorry I let this happen. And I'm not your uncle. You're a man now—you can't call me that no more."

Max paused. Was he being too hard on the kid? "Son, you got a deal of growing-up to do. Just call me Max. Be very careful. Now, I got to go. I got things—dangerous things—to do. Over and out."

At Vancouver Island Naval Base, Admiral Franklin Keating, a fifty-year-old, cart-horse of a man immaculately dressed in full uniform, stood to attention at his desk, a telephone rammed to his ear.

"Jesus fucking H. Christ! What in hell were them scum-suckers playing at down there? Don't you got no fucking security? Shar was the best damn thing that happened to this country since that pimp President Pooley spread his fat ass in the White House."

Max, still wearing his headset, answered with more than a hint of recrimination. "Sorry Frank. I know I should have been with him. I'll never forgive myself."

"Don't blame yourself, Max … Mr. President," said Keating. "No one could have known that bastard Pascalo would go rogue. If you'd been with Janus, they'd have taken you out too. America needs you now. We'll trash this motherfucking scum. Oh, yeah!"

As Keating put the phone down, he looked out of the window to the naval base below. The shipyard was a hive of activity—the likes of which had not been seen since World War II. Whistles and klaxons sounded, heralding a great mustering of sailors, airmen, and marines. Ships were being made ready: guns and aircraft shedding their mothballs.

Cloirina Braganza sat at her desk, pressing the ivory-colored telephone to her ear. Every word Max spoke caused fresh tears to fall from her eyes. But as the news of her love and ambitions shattered around her, her paramount thoughts were of survival. When she answered, there was hardly a tremble in her voice.

"Thank you, Maxwell … you were a true friend to my President. He always spoke well of you. May I come to the funeral?"

Max thought for a moment. An official invitation was out of the question—protocol would never allow it. "I'm sorry. I can't invite you, Cloirina, it wouldn't be fair to BB, but … well, it's a free country."

"It always would have been, Maxwell," she said with a spark of irony. "Whatever you may think of me, Janus was not a tyrant."

"I know that, Cloirina. When this is all over I'll come and see you. How is … everything?"

"Oh, just doodle-dandy. Please do come, Maxwell, please. Until then, what you see is what you get." She replaced the phone, thought for a moment then turned in her chair to face her entire family. Every member was gathered: Walter, other uncles, aunts, her brother, and cousins, all before her like a Senate, listening and watching her every word and gesture, their worried eyes scrutinizing hers.

She stared back, unblinking as she addressed them. "Now we must wait for the scum to settle. Whoever

rises to the top will want to resurrect The Americas …
money, money, money."

There was no comment or reaction as, one by one,
they stood and left the room. Cloirina turned back to
her desk and folded her hands across her stomach,
symbolically protecting the child within.

A semicircle of Senators sat before Pascalo as he
prepared to address the nation. He was standing at the
lectern in five-star general's uniform. A multitude of
reporters and cameramen were at the ready. Beyond
these sat Senators and Congressmen, providing a
nervous, somber audience. The urgent mumbling came
to an abrupt halt as Pascalo raised his hand, indicating
he was about to begin his address.

"Americans … fellow countrymen … lovers of
freedom, since that first engagement on Lexington
Common in 1775—that is what we've been." He paused
for a moment to judge the mood: none was discernable.
"Earlier today, as you've just seen on the screen for
yourselves, myself, Mayor Savarge, Governor Cusac,
and Governor Ford took up the gauntlet cast down by
President Shar … an open, fearless and, yes, bloody
action. Just like all those years ago when we Americans
turned our backs on tyranny … on monarchy."

He stopped again; there was still no indication
of mood. His mind momentarily traveled across the
many miles to the city's military airport. There, at his
command, a fully manned and armed Kaon bomber
waited, in the event of the unthinkable. Were his
well-laid plans going sour? If so, this would be their

contingency. But now there were murmurings from the audience, urging him to continue. Pascalo felt a sudden rise in confidence. Now, he needed to rouse them.

"Monarchs..." he continued, his voice rising theatrically. "Monarchs are for the oppressor, for the imperialist. We are free! Our Constitution demands it. If I have offended, I am deeply sorry ... but I offer no excuse other than my love for America and freedom. If our deed seems horrendous, imagine the alternative."

The audience was still silent. He must win them. "I hear you say Shar was a Great American," his voice now shaking with emotion. "Yes, true, but he was ambitious. Not a bad thing. Again, I hear you say we are all ambitious. But his ambition was heinous, and with it came all those things we'd determined to put behind us. Shar had become enemy of the Republic, the oldest, noblest remaining republic in the world. Were we about to lose that? He had to die! History has shown us that. What we—champions of freedom—did, we did openly for all to see ... the folly of ambition. And, if absolution is too great a burden to put upon you, our fellow free Americans, then by these same hands, so must we perish."

Pascalo detected a slight murmuring: a solitary person clapping, now another, now many. At last, the whole house, Senators, and congressmen were clapping and cheering. Had he done it? Had he swung them? Yes! They had committed, totally. They had symbolically, as in ancient days, raised him aloft on his shield. There could be no turning back for them now—no matter what Tunney would say.

At length, Pascalo held up his hand, commanding his adoring audience to order. "Americans everywhere, grieve … a great man is dead. But also, Americans, rejoice … *tyranny* is dead! The republic lives! And now, with our permission, Maxwell Tunney will deliver Shar's epitaph."

Their reaction to this confirmed their allegiance; they seemed dead set against Max Tunney's right to speak, so venomously did they voice their anger that Pascalo was obliged to pause again.

He raised his hand regally, and there was obedient silence. "As Janus Shar's friend, Max Tunney has that right. This is after all, still a free country. Let him give epitaph to a great, but woefully-misguided, American."

To thunderous applause, Pascalo walked slowly from the lectern and out of the hall, knowing he had them in the palm of his hand.

From within the group of Senators, an angry voice made itself heard over the cheering. "What's Tunney gonna spin out of this? We don't need his gerrymandering! —Quebec."

A second voice rang out. "He's okay; let him speak, for Shar's sake. —Missouri."

Then a third voice. "Why? What's done is done. The king is dead, God save the Republic! Oh, yeah! —Wyoming."

The applause, degenerating to jeering, heralded Maxwell Tunney to the lectern. The crowd pushed forward, catcalling as he took the place that Pascalo had just vacated. Max waited until they had come to some kind of order, and then spoke softly into the microphone.

"General Pascalo called you 'fellow Americans.'" Jeering again.

A menacing figure pushed forward and hurled his words. "What's the matter, Tunney? Don't you like the sound of that? —Nevada."

Another Senator stood and yelled, "Yeah, would you sooner he call us *subjects?* —Utah"

This set off more jeering.

"No, Utah," Max replied calmly. "No, I would not … I'd sooner call you friends … then Americans … then citizens. You are all of these … but most of all friends. A man can live in this world without countrymen, but he cannot live without friends." His tone became slightly more insistent. "Janus Shar was my friend." He raised his voice a little louder. "Pascalo says he was ambitious—you bet your sweet life he was ambitious." His voice became grave, almost menacing. "Pascalo is an honorable man, but Pascalo says Shar was too ambitious…" He paused a moment, and then continued with an incredulous edge to his voice. "Was Janus Shar too ambitious to put together the greatest deal this century has seen: the unification of The Americas?"

The jeering stopped while they considered this. Max sensed their slight mood change. He raised his voice even more. "Yeah, The Americas!" The words were picked up by voices in the audience—he'd hit them in their pockets. "God, The Americas, that sounds good, doesn't it? Well, doesn't it?"

In response, the crowd chanted, "The Americas. The Americas!"

Max now worked the house, striding, microphone in hand, like some mesmerizing evangelist or rock star, punctuating his words with stabbing hand gestures. "Shar saw we were losing our lead … Eurasia, with the Russians on board, was edging us out. With the Latin States, America would once again be number one! But…" He paused, and, only when his audience demanded, did he proceed. "… But Pascalo says he was ambitious, and he and his junta …" He spat out the word as if it were poison, and then paused again. All were now beginning to respond. His hand rose, directing them as a conductor would an orchestra. A palpable hush now enveloped the crowd. "Yes. And his junta are—so you all seem to say—honorable men."

On the avenue outside, Daloris Marshall walked to an armored military vehicle. The driver, Robert, greeted her with a nervous smile.

"The streets are crawling with angry mobs, Ma'am," he said, hoping she would call for back up. "I don't like it. There's no reasoning with them."

"We need to hold order, Robert," she said as she climbed into the vehicle. "We got to show some grit. Now, let's get going—we got some important people to pick up."

Robert shrugged, slammed the vehicle into gear, and sped away.

Maybe Max had played the patriotism card too early, although there did seem to be a turn to them. He reached inside his jacket and dramatically withdrew an envelope, then theatrically made as if deciding whether to read it or not. Not! With a shake of his head, he returned it to his pocket, and continued, "Three times I was able to offer Shar the extra term—approved by all factions of the Senate—and three times he refused it. Three times! That was ambition? When he put together the Canadian deal, did we ..." he let his arm sweep around to include himself and the whole audience, "... say that too was ambitious?"

Max made as if he'd had a change of mind, and again brought out the envelope. He brandished it for all to see, then turned it for the best camera view. "This! This is Shar's proposed manifesto. If he'd gotten the extension, this is what he was going to do. You be the judge of what Shar thought of *his* friends." They seemed to surge forward in their seats, eager to see the document. "And who are his friends?" Again he inserted the orator's never-ending pause for effect. Finally, he punched out at the very top of his voice. "Every last undeserving one of you!"

As if overcome with emotion, he paused again. This time, the envelope was returned a little reluctantly to his pocket. "No, I won't read it now. My ... my heart's not in it. My heart's in the coffin with my friend, with my President. I need a moment."

Though truly choking up, Max still managed to emphasize it somewhat. He theatrically cleared his throat and continued. "That's part of my promise to Pas..." He again choked, and with great emotional strain, managed to spit out the name. "Pascalo!" He gave a cautious, theatrically nervous look over his shoulder, "And I don't want to be accused of being too ambitious."

A mumbling arose from the Senators. *Was this a positive mumbling?* Max was now sure.

An elder statesman rose to his feet. Max nodded, permitting him to speak. "We, the Senate, decide that you should read Shar's letter —Nevada."

Another Senator chipped in. "Yeah. That belongs to the House. We demand to hear it! —Oklahoma,"

A chant arose from both sides of the house: "Read it! Read it! Read it! Read it!"

Max smiled to himself and shouted over the chanting. "What's that? You asking me to break the promise I made to Pascalo?"

"That promise, Mr. President," yelled another Senator, pushing through the ranks, "is unconstitutional. We are not asking!" He gave a quick gauge to determine whether the remaining Senators were in support. The seasoned politician sensed they were, and immediately became bolder. "We are *ordering* you to read it! —Nebraska."

Nebraska had called him Mr. President—not Mr. Vice President—and none had objected. Max smiled inwardly, but on the outside, he offered a troubled expression, giving the impression he was struggling with his conscience. "Well, okay … if it's unconstitutional, and if I'm ordered, I guess I don't have a choice." Emboldened by the Senate's united direction, he seemed to acquire a never-before-seen statesmanship. Some of the more influential Senators nodded to one another sagely and approvingly. His authoritative voice silencing all others, Max continued, "But first, let's take us a look at what Janus Shar was about—that is what Pascalo allowed me to do … on his behalf. He, under the circumstances, felt he could not. What had Shar achieved since he first took over from Pooley's masquerade presidency? What did these honorable men say of him then … that he was ambitious?"

Max allowed the word to hang for a moment, to reverberate around the marble hall. Suddenly, his anger erupted. He screamed the next words so loud that they hit with brute shock. "He pulled our godforsaken nation out of the hands of the receiver! Was that too ambitious?"

He again let his words hang, and in the breathless silence that followed, he scanned along the rows of Senators, scrutinizing each, as if making this a personal reproach. Some stared back, but most were compelled to look away. At length, he calmed and continued in his normal, soft voice.

"Janus Shar breathed life back into a failing dollar, and when Governor Ford tried to sell off part of Mexico to the highest bidder, what did Shar do? Well?"

Max waited, challenging them to make a reply. There were a few troubled mumblings. He continued, affecting a face of reason. "Shar put his own family fortune on the line as collateral, paid off that country's debts, and delivered up its newest state 'New NewMexico', unifying Mexico right down to Nicaragua. And what then did the honorable Pascalo think of Shar?" Max theatrically cupped his ear, challenging them, mocking them. "Well?" Despite rotating his body to include the entire audience, not surprisingly, no one made as much as a whisper.

Around the hall, Senators and spectators were now debating and arguing. Max paid them no heed. "Remember that day? That famous Pascalo bear hug when he was given the Presidential Guard? That Judas smile when he kissed BB's cheek? Would he kiss her now? You betcha he would—if some bunch of gutless Senators was watching!"

He detected definite sounds of a collective mood change. Now was the time. "It seems to me that— through Pascalo—Pooley has got his revenge! Shar was murdered beneath that traitor's portrait. Why in God's name is that abomination still here?"

From the front row, a grey-haired patriarch stood to address his fellow Senators. "What are we waiting for? Burn the damned thing! — Oklahoma."

"Yeah, rip it up and burn it! —Utah."

"Don't talk about it, do it. We demand it! —Idaho."

Max held the envelope above his head, bringing them to order. "You're forgetting the manifesto. You still want to hear it?"

The chant started again: "Read it! Read it! Read it!"

There was deathly quiet as Max slowly opened the envelope. He took out a clip of papers and studied them. At long length, he looked up and out to his eager audience. "Okay, skipping the family niceties. For a whole six months after Shar had finalized his unification of The Americas, there was to be a trade subsidy. It would apply from Prince of Wales, Alaska, through to Tierra del Fuego—of 20 percent to 75 percent." He studied their faces, slowly moving from one to another.

All were greedily hanging onto his every word. "And every man, woman—Jack and Jill—would have gotten an aligned tax resettlement, backdated to the beginning of this tax year… worth 40 per cent!"

At these words, his voice rose to gasps and cheers and thunderous clapping. Now he was forced to shout to make himself heard. "And these Americas would have become totally self-sufficient! A complete land-linked, God-blessed, island commonwealth!" He paused again, theatrically gasping for breath. "Here was a friend. Here was a President! When will we see his like again?"

Max left the lectern to riotous cheering, the papers waving above his head. Pascalo, Savarge, and Cusac watched Max's speech on a small TV.

"Damn!" sighed Pascalo as he and switched off the set. "Okay, contingency plan. We split up at DC … expedite plan B. We each take a bomber and rendezvous at Sonora."

At DC Military Airport, a second Kaon bomber flamed up its massive engine stacks and taxied down the runway toward the first. From the depths of a great hangar, a third bomber was being towed out.

X

Max and Daloris Marshall surveyed Shar's body in shocked silence, where it had been placed in all its bloody gore on the mortuary slab. After an immeasurable passing of time the pathologist unceremoniously began the autopsy.

Max winced as the knife slit open the chest cavity. "There'll be bloody murder in the streets," he whispered. "You must not be seen to take sides, Daloris ... no sides. Just quell the mob until—"

The knife completed its incision—Daloris did not flinch. "Until *what,* Mr. President? What's going to happen? I need to know and I don't have much time. My driver is covertly picking up the police commissioners of DC, New York, and Maryland. I need to—" She was cut off mid-sentence to a bone-cracking rip and an audible displacement of fluids as Shar's sternum was split and his chest cavity wall opened.

"Dear God," Max said. "Look at him!"

"Max!" Daloris took his arm and shook it to get his attention. "Sir! Mr. President! Tell me what's going to happen? I have to leave. I need to know your thoughts, Sir."

Max hardly heard her. "He was my friend, Daloris. My friend."

"Mr. President ..." the pathologist announced without emotion, "... it was the last blow that killed him. It ripped open his heart."

Max put his hands to his temples and yelled to the heavens, "I swear Janus Shar will not be buried until every last one of them rots in godless hell!"

The White House chapel held the chill of death. Max stood to attention beside a solemn Admiral Keating. A marine sergeant, a Presidential Guard, an air force officer, and an army private stood at each corner of the open casket as if petrified in stone. Outside, an unending column of mourners silently waited to file past Janus Shar's corpse.

Max hissed, "Are we ready?"

Keating answered with an affirmative nod.

BB looked positively enchanting in black. It was, after all, her color, matching her raven hair and contrasting her porcelain complexion. She sat in the White House summer suite taking coffee as Max entered. The aide had introduced him as President Tunney. Max didn't like the sound of it—it was never what he wanted. Even the vice presidency had been virtually forced on him. He'd taken it only to be close to Janus—so he could protect him—much good it had done.

"Tea, Mr. President?" Betty asked.

"Don't call me that."

"Oh. Why not? Isn't that what you now are?"

He ignored the loaded question. "We have to talk, Betty."

BB stood, instinctively smoothing her second-skin dress. She strode away from him, and then swished around like a supermodel on a catwalk. "So, Maxwell, how come?"

"How come? How come what?"

"How come they didn't take you, too?"

"Yeah … damned insulting, isn't it?" He gave an ironic smile. "I should have been there with him … sorry."

"I didn't mean … Max, you have nothing to be sorry for." She sat down and poured him a coffee.

"I guess they didn't see me as a threat." Max sat beside her and took the offered coffee. "Huh! They wished!"

"It's too late now, Max. The people will go along with it."

"We'll see. Anyways, what about us? Will the people go along with us?" He searched her eyes for a glimmer of hope.

"Darling, you know the answer to that." She turned away from his look of unbearable loss. "His name is blackened enough."

"Ain't that the truth. I just wanted to love like an ordinary man. Just once in my life—nothing to do with duty or advancement—like an ordinary man."

"Can people like us truly love, Max—us the one-percent, the hierarchy, the elite? Do we give up the right to love for … divinity? Would you trade all this for forty acres and a mule?"

"Yes—if it included you."

"Were we really in love, Max? I've never truly loved before. Did it actually happen?"

"Oh, yes … yes! I won't love again, not like this."

"You will, Max. You will because you are a natural, loving man. You couldn't exist without a beautiful woman to love."

Max put down his cup and then walked toward the door. "I'm in with Wesley." He nodded toward the next apartment. "Afterward, could I come back and say good-bye properly, one last time?"

"Oh Max. Yes, yes!"

Betty was now crying. Max smiled sadly, turned, and walked out.

In the Oval Office, West Wing of the White House—just two days after Janus Shar's assassination—Wesley Shar sat opposite Max, offering the best rendering of an angry face that he could manage. Max was smiling, knowing that the debate was not going to Wesley's liking. Wesley sensed that he was being railroaded, but he was determined to make his mark from the very outset. Max was playing the paternal card.

"I have half the Senate, Maxwell," said Wesley. "By way of my uncle's fortune. Only I can give them The Americas now. I won't—"

"I had no choice, Wes," snapped Max, offering no margin for discussion. "He's threatened to veto Martial Law—leastways delay it. He's in!"

"I won't have a Pooley man among us!" said Wesley, giving as much authority as he could muster. "Henning is a damned mouth on legs!"

"You don't hear good, do ya, Sonny?" Max was deliberately spiteful; he could leave no room for procrastination. Wesley's indecision would result in disaster. "He's part of the Tri-Presidency, and he's in!" Wesley returned a damning stare.

Max shrugged, "Wes, my hands are tied. Yeah, I got my navy, but I need air support. If I don't get that, Pascalo wins. Okay, Henning was a Pooley man, so what? He is the elected representative of the remnant parties. Between them, they hold only a quarter of the vote. The man has zero clout, except veto. We use him to run errands. Either he's in or it costs us a whole week—and by then, it'll be too late. This has to be done quickly. I want them all dead before the first shovel of earth falls on Janus Shar's coffin."

Wesley grimaced. "Don't call me Sonny."

"Then grow the fuck up! Because if Pascalo takes DC, you won't get that chance. You understand what I'm saying?"

"I grew up the moment they told me about my uncle … that's why I didn't run."

"That was commendable. I admire you for that."

"One day, Maxwell, you'll trip over that slippery, silver tongue of yours and we'll stand toe-to-toe."

Max manufactured a mock face of fury, which, after a fleeting second, melted back to his regular smile. "No way! You're young, you're green, and you're goddamn starchy, but … I like you, Wes. That surprises you, right?"

Wesley gave a grudging smile. "No one likes me. I'm unlikable."

"Nuts!" laughed Max. "You're a chip off the old block, Wes. Tell ya what, I'll teach you all I know—for J's sake—if you'll listen, Sonny." He grabbed Wesley's hand, forcing him to shake.

"I will tell you this, Maxwell," said Wesley, removing his hand, "for J's sake, do not underestimate me. I'm a quick learner."

"Sure. Sure you are. Now, I got my list of names." Wesley reluctantly accepted the offered document. Max went on. "Sorry, your brother's amongst them. See, I've written his name in pencil—you can rub it out if you feel you have to."

As Wesley scanned the list of names, the color drained from his already sickly face. "Let it stay. I too have a list—no doubt you'll find a few of your old friends included. We are talking insurrection here, Maxwell. You are aware that this carries the death penalty? It's never been revoked."

"Yes. That was top of the list in your uncle's next term manifesto—ironic isn't it?"

Wesley took a deep breath. "So ... when do we strike?"

"We've already struck! Start to learn, Wes, start to learn."

A squadron of Fusion UCAV—unmanned combat air vehicle—scramjet fighters, flying at Mach-2, closed on the three Kaon bombers. The bombers split up and, under rocket boost, soared to high altitude—out of the range of their oxygen-voracious pursuers.

XI

An armored military vehicle forced its way through the great surge of people. They were now close to riot—some tearful, some furiously protesting, others fighting, breaking into groups and smashing windows and cars—anything to vent their anger.

Daloris Marshall sat in the patrol car next to her driver. Behind them were three city police chiefs: Focard, New York; Corrigan, Richmond; and Chapman, Atlantic City. "Hand me the microphone, Bob," said Daloris. "We have to get through this. I need somewhere high. Where do you suggest?"

Robert handed it to her and shrugged. "Take your pick."

Corrigan leaned his head toward her. "I suggest you orchestrate from here. We got five cars and two choppers awaiting instruction."

"And I'll have another two choppers here in fifteen minutes," Focard added. "Plus we got SWAT teams all over … none seen action yet, thank God."

"Well, I suggest we use the Presidential Guard," said Chapman. "Any chance, Marshall?"

"None! They offered, but President Tunney says no! It's his first direct order. Anyway, it would only incense the mob. No, we just contain things best we can. We need to let some time pass." She picked up the hand microphone:

"Leave the streets!" Outside, her voice boomed out through the car's speaker, over the din of the crowd. "Go to your homes and turn on the TV. Martial Law has been declared. I repeat, leave the streets!"

A stone crashed into the windshield. The glass cracked, but did not smash.

"Jesus Christ!" yelled Focard. "We need to back off—we're just antagonizing them!"

"You want to reconsider that?" said Daloris. "I got people out there and they need my direction."

"The choppers can do that," Focard replied. "I tell you all we're doing is antagonizing them. They're mad as hell, and they don't know who to blame. They'll go for anything or anyone, uniform or not."

Robert twisted in his seat to look out the rear window. "Don't matter no which-ways now. See, the mob's tipped over a truck ... right behind us."

"Christ, they set the fucker alight!" screamed Corrigan, "Forward—go forward!"

The crowd backed away from the flames, forming a semi-circle around the car. Suddenly, a Molotov cocktail smashed onto the windshield and the car erupted in flames.

Inside, Corrigan grabbed at Robert's shoulder. "Get us out of here! Now!"

"I can't. I can't go either way! We got to get out!"

Chapmann, Focard, Corrigan, and Daloris, carrying a hand-held hailer, tumbled from the passenger side of the vehicle. Robert tried to clamber out, but entangled himself on the protruding gearshift.

"Bob!" yelled Daloris. "Get moving now! Quickly!"

"I can't get past!" Robert was close to hysteria. "I have to go my side. I … Jesus! We're on fire! I got to get out!" In one movement, he tumbled into the street from the other side of the vehicle.

Daloris screamed, "Get back! Everybody get back! The car's going to blow! Get back!"

She desperately pushed into the crowd, attempting to reach Robert. He'd rolled away from the flames and scrambled to his feet, but couldn't get around the burning car to join them. Angry voices from the crowd yelled at him.

"You murdering bastard!"

"Get him!"

"Yeah, they're all in it—get him!"

As the mob closed in, Robert put up his arms to protect himself. "Hey, hold it! I'm just a driver. It's nothing to do with me!"

The mob was on him, screaming at him as they beat him. "Murdering bastard!"

Covering up as best as he could, Robert managed to snatch out his wallet. "God's sake! Look! I'm one of you! I'm a Teamster for Christ's sake—a worker!"

A rough-looking man grabbed the wallet. "You bastards are all the same—you got -cards for everything, you fuckin' Nazi!" The man glanced at Robert's ID card, reading the name out loud: "Robert Ford. Hey! This asshole's Bob Ford! He was a goddamn back-shooter! He killed Jesse James."

A man from the mob answered. "Yeah—and Charley Ford killed Shar."

"Jesus H. Christ," said the first man. "Ford's one hell-of a bad name to have today."

Robert tried to pull away. "I'm nothing to do with them. It's just a name—that's all!"

The man looked at Robert, then took in the mob and gave a menacing grin. "One Ford's as good as another?" The mob closed in. Robert went down under them. After a few moments, they moved away. The flames from the burning patrol car had reached the flames of the truck. An impenetrable wall of fire left Daloris and the police chiefs isolated. They could do nothing but stare into the growing inferno as it closed over Robert's lifeless body.

High in the stratosphere above the Gulf of Mexico, the three Kaon bombers rejoined formation. Their rocket-boost ability for high-altitude flight had given them some respite from the fighters. Now they had to lose altitude and find air themselves or squander the boosters. The turbo-ramjet engines of the three bombers screamed in unison as they gulped the oxygen-thin atmosphere.

Inside the first bomber, Cusac, wearing high-altitude suit and helmet, sat as part of the crew. The flight captain pointed to a radar screen.

"Damn! We got visitors, Governor. More scramjets … we can't outrun them mothers down here—there's three of us, why the hell they pick on us?"

Cusac looked at the screen and then rolled his eyes. "Right, Son, get it up. We got the wings for it. Scramjets don't drink thin air."

The captain pulled back the stick and the craft rammed higher into the stratosphere. Sir," he said without emotion, "we have a missile locked onto us!"

"Higher," yelled Cusac. "Damn it, Son! Hit the thermosphere if you have to."

The captain gave Cusac a questioning look, and then spoke to the crew through his helmet microphone. "Captain to crew: Lock helmets, no smoking. Houston, we are about to take a giant step into space."

Cusac smiled, realizing the futility of the action. "Captain, what do ya say we skim the stratosphere then jackknife into a dive? Any of them assholes follow; they'll break their goddamn backs. Well?"

"You wanna fly this thing, Sir?" growled the captain.

"Only if you can't cut it, Son. Use up the rest of the rocket boost."

"Sir, yes, Sir!"

In the second bomber, Pascalo sat aft with the navigator, radio operator, and Terence, who was looking extremely nervous.

"Any coffee, Terry?" said Pascalo. "I need something to keep me awake."

Terence stood, welcoming the distraction. "Lordy! You can sleep in this? I'll go and see, Sir … the altitude we're at, it'll probably float right out of the cup."

Pascalo smiled. "And if I am asleep, Terry, when you come back, just leave me. Okay?"

Terence nodded and moved off. As he made his way to the compact galley, the radio operator handed him a message.

"This just came through. I … I've decoded it. The general's wife … you'd better read it … it's not confirmed. Will you tell him … or shall I?" Without waiting for an answer, he pushed the note into Terence's hand, and turned back to his radio.

As Terence read the note, he wept openly. When he got back to Pascalo, he found him asleep. He left him sleeping; there would be time enough. Now he could wait for confirmation.

Cusac's bomber was now flying vertically. It had all but exhausted its rocket booster.

"Incoming rocket impact, thirty seconds, Sir," the captain said calmly. "Sorry, we haven't reached our required parabola. Shall we start our descent?"

Cusac looked at the captain. "Son," he said with a hint of humor in his voice, "have you ever seen the play, *Hobson's Choice*?"

The captain looked bemused.

"Dive, Son. Dive, dive, dive! Yaaa-hoooo!"

The bomber momentarily hung in space, neither rising nor falling, then plummeted with incredible velocity. Vapor contrails streamed from its engines as they flamed up and gulped in the thin air. A missile exploded. The bomber rocked, but continued on its way.

Close to passing out from the G-force, Cusac managed a half-constructed smile. "Ha! We … beat … the fucker."

"Sir! We've taken flak! Mayday! May—shit! No radio!"

Cusac leaned back into his seat. "Take her up again, Captain. We're sitting ducks down here."

The captain's eyes told Cusac that there was no hope. "I'm going to take a little nap," said Cusac, closing his eyes, "Wake me if something important happens. Take her up, Son."

"Yes Sir… high as you like, Sir."

"Keep pouring till I say when."

The bomber fired its remnant second booster, ramming the craft into vertical, higher and higher until the rocket flamed out. It momentarily hung, frozen in time, then fell back into its own contrail. Two missiles homed in … a huge explosion, then blackness.

XII

It was early evening as the second Kaon bomber landed safely at Sonora Military Airport, Mexico. Pascalo was met by a group of high-ranking militaries, led to a waiting vehicle, and then driven at high speed to his HQ. Safely settled inside, he gave the war council his stratagem for the now unavoidable conflict. He finished his address to animated applause. An aide entered and delivered a message into Pascalo's hand and stood waiting at attention for an answer.

Pascalo quickly read the message. "It's Mayor … or should I say General Savarge, safely landed. If you gentlemen don't mind, I'll see him alone."

In confident spirits, the generals began leaving the room, passing Savarge, now dressed in a five-star general's uniform, coming in. They greeted him cordially.

"Well done, General!"

"Glad you made it, Owen."

"Good old American kick-ass."

When Pascalo and Savarge were alone, Pascalo closed and locked the door.

"Cusac?" Savarge asked. "He never made it?"

"Affirmative," answered Pascalo.

Savarge expelled a deep breath. "Damn!"

"Where are your troops, Owen?" Pascalo asked with an air of sarcasm. "They should be here. Are they here? Where's B Company?"

"Sorry … it's gonna take a day—"

"I was told two!" Pascalo's voice had a chilling edge. "The hell you think you're playing at? Your damned penny-pinching will get us hung."

"Just a goddamn minute!" Savarge thrust his face into Pascalo's. "What are you accusing me of? You think I'm on the make here? Is that it?"

"You were to ready all the southern battalions—not wait to see the outcome! Is it done? Goddamn it, man, this was crucial. Crucial!"

"I didn't think it necessary. We told you not to let Tunney speak. I thought—"

"Damn you!" yelled Pascalo. "You've been lining your pockets with our lives … those troops were crucial!"

Savarge pulled his pistol and pointed it at Pascalo. "You self-righteous, pompous fucking prig! Are you calling me a crook?"

Pascalo thrust his chest onto the pistol barrel. "When we stabbed Shar, it wasn't for coin, and it wasn't for gain—it was for America!"

"I'm not having this shit! Who the hell do you think you're talking to? I've seen twice as much service as you … active service. These medals didn't come with the fucking uniform. I strike the battle plans … me!"

"No you don't!"

"I say yes." Savarge raised the pistol to Pascalo's head. Say no one more time and I'll waste you, here and now, so help me! I'll—"

"You haven't the belly for it."

"You fucking kidding me?"

"Oh, oh!" Pascalo rolled his eyes like a vaudeville actor. "My legs are shaking."

Savarge gave and incredulous look, "I don't fucking believe this."

"Go wave your gun at your troops," said Pascalo. "That is—if you can find them. See if you can make them tremble."

Savarge, speechless, cocked the pistol. Pascalo let rip a bellow of laughter. "Hah! So I'm to beg for mercy, is that it? You are a standing joke, Owen. You know that? You were a far better mayor than you ever were a general. You—a better soldier than me? Show me your men!"

The gun wavered. "You got it wrong, Richard. I said I've seen more service—I never said I was the better soldier."

"What the hell?"

Savarge uncocked the pistol, lowered it, and then offered it to Pascalo. "Here, take it. Use it if you think that badly of me."

Pascalo looked at the weapon for a few moments and then turned away. "For God's sake, put it away."

Savarge expelled a breath. "Anyways, Richard, I've got my troops on standby. They're ready to go in twelve hours. Whoever said two days must have misunderstood. Let me speak to them ... let's not fall out over this. Save your stoicism for Tunney."

Pascalo turned back, and smiled. *"So now I'm a stoic—and I didn't know it."* He said the words to make a rhyme.

Savarge put his thumb and forefinger together, almost touching and offered the gesture.

Pascalo shrugged. "I take it that's how close I came to you killing me?"

"No, you didn't come close at all. This is how funny your fucking joke was." He pointed the gun at the floor and pulled the trigger ... a metallic click. "I never carry a loaded gun, not since I once near blowed my balls off." He offered his hand—his anger now subsided. "Come on, Richard, shake on it?"

Pascalo grabbed the hand Roman style, pulling them face-to-face. "I jumped the gun, Owen. Sorry, I had some bad news ... Mercedes."

He moved to his desk and started flipping through papers. Savarge waited for more, and then prompted. "Richard ... Mercedes?"

At the desk, Pascalo had found the document he wanted and intently scanned the single page. "The report is ... sketchy."

Savarge gasped aloud. "Mercedes is—"

"Dead! We're waiting confirmation, but—"

"How, for God's sake? Dead?"

"Did you know she'd tried once before? The blade—ironic isn't it? They found her dead with the TV running. She'd seen it—everything. Mercedes is our first casualty of war."

Savarge, still holding the pistol, placed a hand on Pascalo's shoulder. It was promptly brushed off. "We won't speak of this again, Owen." He reached into the desk drawer and brought out a bottle and glasses.

"Scotch?" He calmly poured two whiskies, sipped one, and offered the other to the still-shocked Savarge.

Savarge attempted to take it, but still had the gun in his hand. He stared at the big black automatic and gave an incredulous smile. "God, how did I escape you killing me, provoking you when—"

"You offered me an empty gun, remember?"

Savarge shrugged, spun the gun on his finger, cowboy style, and tripped it back into its holster. Pascalo nudged the glass toward him again. This time he took it, swallowing its contents in a single mouthful.

"Shit! I don't think I ever needed a drink so much in my life." He held out the glass and Pascalo poured a generous refill.

An urgent knocking on the door was followed by Terence's strained voice. "Sir! A message." Pascalo unlocked the door admitting his aide, brandishing a printout. "Sir?"

"Read it for me, would you, Terence?"

Terence took a deep breath—this wasn't going to be easy. "It's from Governor Ford, Sir. Tri-Presidents Maxwell Tunney, Wesley Shar, and Joseph Henning are mustering a task force off Vancouver Island. Martial Law has been declared and twenty Senators arrested … ex-Pooley men, mostly."

"Is that all?" Pascalo was icy cool.

"Um … well, no Sir … I have another message … Sir, you'd best hear it alone. I received it on the aircraft, but then it wasn't confirmed … now it is."

"Read it out, Terence." Pascalo smiled. "It's all right."

"It's confirmation … your wife, Sir … she's …"

"Dead. Mercedes is dead. Say it, Terence."

Terence was now openly weeping. "Yes, Sir. Dead, Sir … I'm so sorry."

"It's okay, Terrence. I just wanted to hear it from someone else's lips."

"She'd sent me out to find you, Sir … I shouldn't have left her … I couldn't get back … impossible. I'm so bitterly, bitterly sorry." He covered his tearful eyes and hurried from the room.

Pascalo waved the thought away. "So, Owen, Vancouver Island, it is. What say we have one more drink, then go get them?"

Savarge considered for a moment. "I say we wait, Richard. Let them find us. We just sit tight and wait it out. Tunney's a sailor; he's got no land legs."

"No." Pascalo studied a wall map of North America, "I say you take them while they're still mustering. And me … I fly on to DC, enter the capital victoriously, leading the Presidential Guard in triumph." He spoke now with just the hint of a conspiratorial grin. "The parade is already arranged."

Savarge didn't share his smile. "My way is best. Tunney has to move his carriers all the ways down to San Diego before his scramjets are in range. That'll give us time. God's sake, Richard, you don't take a shit-fight to a fucking skunk!"

Pascalo winced at the crudity of the remark. "What you say makes good sense, Owen, but what I say makes better. Strike now!" He slapped the map. "The longer we leave it, the more he can gather to his side. I say we strike the headless chicken."

"Three-headed chicken, you mean."

"Exactly!" said Pascalo. "They think that a coalition Tri-Presidency will give focus, but by the time they finish arguing over who wears whose hat, it'll be over—if we act!" Again, he thumped the map. "We use my air strike-force. We catch them on the hop … Cape Flattery, as they muster. We've seen their fleet; we outnumber them, two to one. You fly and pick up our fleet in the Pacific, at Point Conception—I had them placed as an expedient—on manoeuvres. Have B company rendezvous—that'll save that day you lost—agreed? Agreed?"

"Okay," said Savarge, far from convinced, "Agreed." He saluted, turned, and left the room without a further word.

Pascalo flopped down on a leather chesterfield and stretched out his legs. He was tired, not just from lack of sleep, just tired. He rubbed his weary eyes, but no sooner had he closed them then there was a knocking on the door. "Damn!" He kept his eyes closed. Maybe if he ignored it, it would go away. The knocking came again. "Come!" he reluctantly called out.

The door opened and Janus Shar calmly stepped in. "You've invited me in unseen, over your threshold, Richard! Tut, tut, tut. I could be the devil himself."

Pascalo recognized the voice. His eyes sprang open. "You!"

"Yes, me … come to see you … come for one of your famous bear hugs. Best be careful though, I'm not yet ascended, a little bit bloody. Well, what do you say?"

Pascalo leapt up, knocking over a chair. "You!"

Shar sighed. "No hug? Oh, what disappointment. So, nothing to say, Richard?"

"Dear God." Pascalo shook his head, not so much in answer—more to clear his brain. "I'm dreaming!"

"Yeah, Richard, I reckon that must be it … what you see, is …" Shar indicated his bloody body and smiled. "So, disappointment, is it?"

More knocking, insistent knocking: Shar turned, walked to the door. "Well, I must leave. People to see, places to go … that's my new saying." The door opened, wiping the specter away. Pascalo blinked. Terence stood in the open doorway, peering around the room.

"Sir? I thought I heard talking."

"Sure you heard talking! I was talking to myself. I'm going mad … that get your stamp of approval?"

Terence looked bewildered. "Sir? I—"

"Sorry, Terence … it's okay." Pascalo righted the overturned chair that the shocked aide was staring at. "I'm overtired." He returned to the chesterfield. "Give me an hour, and then wake me. Tomorrow could get a tad busy."

XIII

Off the coast of California the two fleets met—a fierce battle raged. Air-to-air and sea-to-air missiles, and aerial dogfights: VTJs hanging, waiting for incoming ATAs, then hurling up-and-away out of range … the bizarre tactic reminiscent of archaic computer games.

At this point, Max's forces looked to be taking a beating. Just as victory for the conspirators seemed all but won, a second task force emerged out of the morning mist. The conspirators' fleet was caught in a logistical nightmare. Hoping to follow on his earlier success, Savarge had ordered his B squadron of VTJs to arm with air-to-air missiles, and they were ready to go. However, in the middle of the battle, intelligence had come through suggesting that Max was expecting a second fleet to enter the theatre. Savarge had no choice but to order his B squadron to stand down and be refitted with bombs and air-to-ship torpedoes. Simultaneously, his A squadron—the VTJ flying-wing defending his flank—returned to their carriers for rearming and refueling. This caused a disastrous bottleneck in the air lanes surrounding the conflict.

At that precise moment, Max's second fleet appeared. Preparations for a counterstrike had continued, but Savarge's carriers were caught on two fronts. All that could be done was to clear the decks of B squadron to make room for the incoming A squadron. One after another, VTJs were either retracted into the bowels of the ship's hangars or simply jettisoned over the side of the decks into the sea, anything to make space for the queue of hovering jets.

With the remnant of B squadron now below decks, A squadron was quickly massed on the decks and fueling and rearming begun. The situation was now desperate. Savarge gave the order to launch when ready. On the flight decks, most jets were in position with engines flamed up. The fleet began turning into the wind. Within five minutes, all jets would launch. Just five minutes—who would have dreamed that the tide of battle would shift completely in such a brief interval of time?

Visibility was good. The air officer flapped a white flag, and the first of the VTJs lifted into the air. At that instant, a radar operator screamed, "Incoming scramjets!"

Savarge's forces managed a few frantic bursts of hail-fire with GAU-Purge Gatling guns, but it was too little, too late. The fighters came in so rapidly that they were virtually invisible to the laser range finders. The fleet's decks were strafed with a blanket of fire and shrapnel. Only the first of the VTJs—those already launched—survived. The rest were dead on the decks.

Savarge sat at his desk in his war room, staring at the field phone in his hand. He closed his eyes and ran the cold metal handset across his forehead. He drew a deep breath and made the call. As it connected, he gave the information without emotion.

Half a continent away, from his armored tank outside Washington, Pascalo gasped into his field phone. "Where in the hell did they come from?"

At his desk, the phone shouldered to his ear, Savarge furiously sorted through a pile of maps. "Cape... Disappointment. Ever heard of it? Intelligence didn't see the second fleet—the goddamn place is always shrouded in fog." He screwed the map into a ball and threw it to the floor in defeat. "We should have waited, Richard, made him come to us." He pulled out his pistol. "This time my gun's loaded." He lifted his head and placed the weapon to his temple, dropping the phone to the desk.

Pascalo, on the other end of the line, heard the shot. He lowered the phone and closed his eyes. Immediately the dream with Shar's words came back to him. "Yeah, Richard, that must be it. Disappointment, then."

Pascalo turned to the tank crew. "Okay men, out—show's over! That's an order, out, and take cover—go!"

Outside the vehicle, the crew emerged and dashed for cover. The great tank had been swathed with stars and stripes flags and banners for a triumphant entry into the capital. Pascalo now emerged from the turret to survey the remnants of his army. Suddenly, as if from nowhere, a ring of jump jets lowered and hovered above him. He smiled at the irony. "Disappointment it is, Janus." He quickly dropped back into the tank and secured the hatch. After a few moments, an internal explosion blew the turret clear off. Thick black smoke coiled upward.

When Max, Wesley Shar, and Keating arrived, the fire was long out. They stood together looking at the smoldering tank.

"So," said Keating, "that's it, then?"

Wesley looked away toward the capital, to the prize. "That is it—and for what?"

"I'll tell you for what," said Max. "He was the only one … not like the others, not greed, not envy … it was for America—the noblest reason in the world."

The streets of Washington were crowded for the funeral procession. A huge picture of Janus Shar was carried before the gun-carriage hearse; behind it was the obligatory saddled horse, riderless except for a pair of riding-boots set backward in the stirrups. Max, BB, and Wesley Shar headed the cars carrying the many dignitaries. Max looked straight ahead, not wanting to see the weeping faces. Nevertheless, some irresistible force compelled him to look into the crowd—to the eyes of Cloirina Braganza. She stood in a group of foreign dignitaries.

Max thought that she was truly beautiful as she stared through tearful eyes. He was about to look away when their eyes momentarily locked. She gave a slight, but unmistakable, seductive smile. In that one look, in spite of everything, Max felt his blood rising.

Book Two

'What's brave, what's noble,
let's do it after the high Roman fashion,
and make death proud to take us.'
—Antony and Cleopatra

I

Max Tunney leaned back and rested. He allowed his body to sag. It was not something that he would normally do—not under any circumstances. He was proud of his youthful physique and, like any high school jock, would suck in his stomach in the company of pretty girls and attractive women—or men if they were deemed rivals in any way. However, Max was among friends, naked and unashamedly sweating. Most importantly, his lower body was completely covered with steam. No one could actually see the slight potbelly that, in spite of an hour every day spent in the gym, was fighting his six-pack. He was, after all, pushing fifty. *Everything goes south after fifty,* he thought as he contemplated his navel. He'd forgotten where he'd heard that.

Max was seated in the Senate steam room on Capitol Hill. Beside him were Wesley Shar and Joseph Henning, co-members in the Tri-Presidency, struck in accordance with the recent, state-of-emergency amendment to the American Constitution. Opposite were his two naval aides, Hermann and Onis. Except for the odd, strategically placed towel, all five were completely naked.

Hermann, a huge man of mixed race, leaned forward and tipped a ladleful of water onto the brazier, producing a loud hissing and a voluminous cloud of vapor. The group was momentarily enveloped.

"Wound deeply?" said Hermann.

Max shrugged. "How about sever?"

Onis shook his head. "Nope."

"Why not?" Max was slightly annoyed. "If I severed your goddamn head, wouldn't you be wounded deeply?"

Onis brushed the sweat from an arm, making a slapping noise. "Well, it still ain't that."

As the steam subsided, Wesley Shar threw Max a mocking smile. "Chop?"

"Chop is wrong too, smart-ass," Max snapped. "Chop is sever."

Onis confirmed the negative with a smile and a shake of his head. He was enjoying this: the three most important men in the world were eating out of his hand. Not bad for an immigrant boy from Hell's Kitchen. "Nope!"

Henning laughed and eyed Onis. "Slice?"

"Slice is not deeply." Max, now on the edge of boredom, glanced at Onis. "Wrong, right?"

"Right, wrong." Onis confirmed the negative, scoring a grudging smile from Max. He laughed. "Come on, superior intellects, come on!"

"Rupture!" Hermann said.

"Nope!"

"How many letters?" demanded Wesley.

the morons. How about you, Max, did you know the answer?" Max was lost in thought. Onis asked again, "Hey, doodle dandy, how about you?"

Max's mind was elsewhere—Onis' words had evoked a distant memory—he repeated them in his head. They transported him back six months to the assassination of his friend and President. As he stared into the clouds of steam, Janus Shar's smiling face emerged.

"Why, Max," said the specter. "Nice of you to ask. I'm just doodle dandy, how about you?" Janus Shar stepped nobly out of the steam and stood in front of Max, awash with blood from a dozen weeping wounds. He reached out a bloody hand for Max to shake. Now Pascalo, Cusac, Savarge, and Ford appeared out of the steam, all with bloody ice picks in their hands.

"Hey, Tunney! How about you?" Onis' words cut through the fantasy and Max jolted awake. The specters evaporated into the steam. Max shook his head, tossing off a spiral of sweat. "What? Yeah, I knew that one... and don't call me Tunney—unless you're tired of your soft job, jerk-off. It's 'Sir' to you."

"I don't call no one, Sir," said Onis, "not even my own father, less it's navy—and I'd trade my soft job for your softer job, Mr. Vice President."

"Mr. President to you, plebe."

"But Joint-President to me," Wesley said.

Henning laughed. "Yeah—and to me."

Onis crumpled up the newspapers and shoved them under the seat. "Well, you three starlets are running out of time. Your six months sufferance is just about up."

Henning looked at Max. "Do we have to put up with these two scumbags of yours?"

Max winked at Onis. "They make me laugh. We need them—with our three sour faces around."

Hermann raised a clenched fist. "Yeah, that's right, you need us. And, as my partner here just pointed out, time is running out. So you three little maids from school better hitch up your drawers and start campaigning."

"That's right," said Onis, backing up Hermann. "You guys put up with us because we watch your asses. So don't go breaking our balls or we might fall asleep on the job."

Hermann glanced at Onis: the conspiratorial notion clicked simultaneously. They both leapt to their feet and started singing, Kiki Dee and Elton John style, "Don't go breaking our balls. (Onis in falsetto) I couldn't if I tried. (Both) Honey, if we get restless? (Onis) Baby, we're not that kind"

Wesley sighed impatiently to Max as the buffoonery continued. "Well, I don't find this local-boy camaraderie amusing. This country is still in mourning."

Onis stared at Max, sat back down, and then slowly pulled a huge pistol—still neatly wrapped in the plastic bag that he'd been so carefully sitting on—from between his legs. He pointed it at arm's length, finger resting through the plastic onto the trigger.

"Yeah, well morning has broken, Senators," he growled with a cutting edge to his voice, "and lunch is being served… and one of you three is main course. Leastways *I'm* doing my job."

Hermann laughed, pointed at the weapon. "Why the hell you got that thing in here, boy?"

"Doing my job—like you should be doing your job, jackass."

Hermann laughed again. "Why the goddamn plastic bag?"

"How long you been in the navy, boy? Tradition—always keep your powder dry."

"Long enough to outrank you, Petty Officer," Hermann yapped, jokingly pulling rank, "And that thing would fire under water for Christ sakes. So why?"

Onis gave Hermann an incredulous look. "So I don't have to clean the fucker. That okay with you? And you only outrank me when we're crew, smartass."

"Hey, buddy—we ain't never crew ... we're ... the elite, the Immortals. Right, Max?"

Max stood up, disinterested. "I've had enough of this." He gathered his towel around himself, and started to leave. "I'm out of here."

"Things getting too hot, Maxwell?" asked Wesley. "Going for a little drink?"

"A little drink?" Max took a deep breath; he'd been on the edge for a long time, "No. I'm going for a big drink—and a big woman. I'd ask you to join me, but I know neither is to your taste ... Sonny."

They all laughed, except Wesley.

Wesley threw his towel over his shoulder and raised his head. "That remark was uncalled for, spiteful and—let me add—politically unacceptable!"

Max rolled his eyes in exasperation. "Christ's sake, Wes, it was a joke. Get it? Joke—five letters, beginning with J and ending with ha ha?"

"Well, it didn't sound like a joke. A joke is supposed to be funny to everybody—not just a select audience."

"I told you before, Wes, I like you. I've liked you since you was a snot-nose kid, when I was Uncle Max… remember?"

"Yes, I remember. But that was a long time ago, Maxwell. We've crossed that Rubicon—there's no going back there."

Max shook his head ruefully. "I hear what you're saying. We ain't gonna fall out, are we, kid?"

Wesley sighed. "No. Sorry, Maxwell, I seem to have lost my sense-of-humor lately. I haven't laughed for … God, I don't know."

"Yeah … Janus was more like your father than an uncle. We all miss him, Wes, but I guess you miss him most."

Max had always had a genuine regard for Wesley, which at times, like now, was, to say the very least, trying. He wiped his face with the towel. "Hey, Wes, why don't you come to Vegas with us—the boys and me? They got Jerry Lewis, he'll make you goddamn laugh. You too, Joe. The three Presidents, the three Amigos, the three Musketeers—Vegas or bust! What do ya say? A week on the town? One for all, and all for me … then I'm off to Brazil."

"Jerry Lewis," said Wesley, hardly interested, "is he still alive?"

Max laughed. "Alive? No, not really. Not as we know it—but he is funny!"

"No thanks, Maxwell. I don't think so."

Henning stood up and tipped some more water on the stones. "Hell, I'm game. My people will be glad to have me out of their hair for a week."

Max pulled his towel around him and turned to Onis and Hermann. "I take it you two are game?"

"Yo!" the answer came in unison.

Wesley gave a disapproving scowl. "Watch yourself in Brazil, Maxwell. That Braganza woman—from what I've heard of her, she'll eat you alive."

Hermann waggled his tongue lewdly. "Hmmmmm … he should be so lucky." Max laughed and Wesley looked bemused.

"Yeah!" roared Onis. "That's if you don't mind stretch marks and the sweet aroma of diaper."

Wesley looked away, affronted. "Oh, for God's sake!"

They all laughed, except Wesley.

II

Caesar's Palace was crowded for the middle of the week. Somehow the news had leaked out—as it always did—that the Presidents were to make a visit. Max and Henning sat encircled by a ring of identically dressed security men wearing the obligatory sunglasses and doing their damnedest to look like security men. This entailed ignoring the cabaret, and staring threateningly at everyone and everything.

Sitting within the encircled group were three attractive women and an entourage of discreetly placed personal bodyguards, including Onis and Hermann. Max was engrossed with one of the women, Vena, a vivacious redhead. On stage, Jerry Lewis was slamming through his routine.

Lewis now looked at Max and gave an exaggerated look of surprise. "Hey, folks." His high-pitched voice winced into the microphone. "I see we got two of the Tri-Presidents in tonight. Hi, Mr. Henning! Hi, Max! You having a nice time? Ladies treating you good?"

Max gave a regal wave to Lewis and to the audience, and nodded confirmatively toward Vena.

"I can recommend that little redhead," continued Lewis, winking to the audience, "poisonally!"

Vena leapt to her feet and hurled her words back at him. "Go frig yourself, Jerry Jerk-Off! I ain't never slept with you in my life."

Lewis screwed his brow as if straining to remember. "Never! Is that so? Why not? I'm Jerry Lewis. I'm famous! Hey, whatcha doing after the show, Baby?"

Max laughed and the audience laughed. Vena, still standing, looked around the palatial ballroom, realizing that everybody was laughing and clapping for her. She smiled and curtsied, accepting the applause in good humor.

She yelled back at Lewis, "Ar, get out of here." She gave another mocking curtsy and sat down. Max leaned over and whispered in her ear, causing her to shriek with laughter.

In the Jade Palace, Cloirina Braganza, in the last throes of childbirth, shrieked in agony. After much screaming and pushing, the matronly midwife lifted the newborn child and held it protectively away from Cloirina.

"Let me see my little President," Cloirina gasped from within the gas-and-air mask. "Now!"

"Si, si, Ma'am." The midwife slightly lowered the child.

"So I can see him, you fool!" Cloirina gulped another breath of gas. "Nearer!"

The woman held the child nearer, but out of Cloirina's reach. "Si. But first I must—"

"I said now!"

The midwife held the child closer.

"Closer, closer!" Cloirina pulled the mask from her face and studied the child. "Is a boy, yes?"

"Si, si, *beleza… bonito*, big boy."

"Then give him to me."

The midwife hesitated. "You must be careful with him."

"Give him to me!" Cloirina snatched the child— umbilical still attached—and spoke close into his face. "Janus Shar Junior, how do you do?" She put her ear to the child's mouth, as if listening. "What's that you say? Just doodle dandy!" The midwife attempted to take the child, but Cloirina held onto him. "You will have it all, my little President. I promise … The Americas!"

The midwife forcibly took back the child and proceeded to cut the cord. Cloirina smiled and closed her eyes.

In the annexe outside the birthing room, the assembled Braganza family sat waiting. The door opened and the midwife popped her head out.

"*Mascolino. Beleza, bonito*," she cried with exuberance. "Big boy. *Beleza!*"

Walter Braganza, Cloirina's uncle and President of Brazil, stood up and shook his head dismissively before storming out of the room. Cloirina's brother Michael looked despondently at the floor. After a few moments, Walter returned to his seat and, after composing himself, proceeded to clap his hands. Michael followed—and the rest obediently joined in.

In the birthing room, Cloirina heard the clapping. She was not fooled by her family's seemingly warm reception for this heir-apparent, but, for the moment, she was safe. It was paramount to keep alive the dream of The Americas—and for this she needed Maxwell Tunney.

The child, now washed, powdered, and wrapped in a blanket, was content in his mother's arms. Cloirina was smiling, playing the doting mother, full of joy for her firstborn. However, this genuine feeling of affection for her son was overlaid by a deeper, darker feeling, one of impending triumph! He was the catalyst to achieve her lofty ambitions.

In the White House, the mood was somber, as all factions of the Senate assembled. An emergency State-of-the-Republic summit had been demanded by the two main parties and the remnant coalition, and was now in progress.

Wesley Shar stood erect at the lectern, doing his best to offer a figure of macho forcefulness. "—Again it is left to me, while Tunney, Henning, and their wastrel rat-pack idle their time away in … wherever. So … it is left to me." He paused to survey the many tiers of Senators. None gave him much credence; it was patently obvious that his reputation had preceded him. "Well, I tell you this, I am getting tired of being the fall guy." He blew out his chest and scowled menacingly at them. "It's been six months since my uncle was, shall we say, deprived of office. And where was Maxwell Tunney then?" Again he studied them, but few were even bothering to pay attention. In spite of his lofty title, Tri-President, he was still deemed the undercard on the speakers' list. Some of his audience murmured, whether in agreement or otherwise, he couldn't tell. He lifted his voice a decibel as he continued. "Now you say it is he who must rekindle my uncle's dream. Why? Why him? Because he brought Canada onboard?" One of the front-row Senators jabbed his hand in the air for attention. Wesley turned to him. "Yes, Idaho?"

The Senator stood, cleared his throat, and directed his words at Wesley. "I don't think you're being fair to Tunney." He looked from side to side for support. "Max loved Janus Shar like a father." Mumbles of endorsement came from both sides, giving the man added confidence. He continued with an edge to his voice. "And where were you when the President needed you? In goddamn Alaska! —Idaho." With that, he sat dramatically.

An elderly Senator angrily chipped in. "The hell do you mean, *goddamn* Alaska? I represent that wonderful, bountiful state. Apologize, Sir. —Alaska."

Idaho stood again. "Archie, I didn't mean nothing derogatory, and you damn well know it. I just meant—"

"Apologize. Apologize!" yelled Alaska from his seat.

As Idaho was forced to sit, a halfhearted chant was picked up by the Alaskan Senator's supporters. "Apologize! Apologize!"

"Go to hell," growled Idaho without bothering to stand. "Better still, go to goddamn Alaska." His words were greeted with howls of laughter from his supporters.

The Alaskan Senator again rose to his feet, beamed a smile to his supporters. Having scored his point, he took a bow and sat down.

Another Senator stood. Wesley tipped his head. "Nebraska?"

Nebraska politely nodded back. "I say if Tunney can deliver, then, hell, let it stand ... status quo. Remember, Tunney has met Cloirina Braganza—and you haven't. And, as I'm informed, they seemed to have a rapport. —Nebraska."

"Yeah, you would know that—you got your nose up everybody's rapport. —Utah."

There were howls of laughter from both sides. Wesley Shar, however, did not share the humor. "Thank you, Utah," he said, rising above the puerile banter. "Most eloquently put. Carry on, Nebraska."

The Senator for Nebraska peered around until he found Utah. "It's my business to have my nose in everybody's rapport. I run a goddamn newspaper. Ever heard of the *Nebraska Times*? —Nebraska."

"Oh yeah! And how is the family business doing since you made Senator? —Utah."

Nebraska turned back to Wesley and continued with difficulty over the laughter. "As I was saying, Mr. President, Tunney has a way with women, nobody can deny that. But with this continuing procrastination, The Americas deal stands idle. What I'm saying is, what Janus Shar started, hopefully, President Tunney can resurrect." Nebraska sat down then bobbed up again, quickly adding, "—Nebraska.'

The laughter and jeers continued as he again took his seat.

Wesley scanned the packed hall for the pockets of dissent. "Yes, laugh," he said, giving the instigators a look of contempt. "That's what the rest of the world is doing—laughing. At us! America has become a joke—a dirty joke! My uncle is turning in his grave!"

He stopped and stared at a randomly chosen few, as if to commit them to some mental list. The laughter stopped. After a lengthy silence, he continued. "When Janus Shar was alive, the world took notice—now it laughs. When Janus Shar was alive, the world trembled at the mention of the name, America—now it laughs!"

A voice called, "Tunney's there already—it's too late to call him back. Let's just see what he comes up with. He did it for Canada, remember?"

"Yes, Nebraska. We shall see. As you so rudely and anonymously, point out, Tunney is there. And when he fails and the world gets another American dirty joke to laugh at—and he will fail—then I will go and pick up the pieces. Nebraska says remember. Well, I too say remember. I remember whose money it took to set up this deal. Not America's—Janus Shar's! He put my family's fortune on the line. And also remember this, Nebraska—and all you Senators and businessmen living off the fat of that deal—I inherited the bulk of that fortune." He paused, letting the drama build. "So now you owe me! And remember this also, Nebraska, I can call in that loan… any time I choose!"

As the full implications of Wesley's words sank in, the ashen-faced Senators looked to each other in dread.

Cloirina paraded naked in front of a full-sized mirror, under the embarrassed gaze of her two maids, who stood patiently waiting to dress her. After examining herself from every angle, her ample hips, her slightly stretch-marked stomach and her swollen breasts—the legacy of a healthy childbirth—she allowed them to start. Eager to cover her nakedness, the servants zealously squeezed her into a corset.

"Es too tight, Ma'am," said the older maid. "I loosen it?"

"Don't you dare," hissed Cloirina. "I need to look … natural. I won't be weak. No brassiere."

The younger maid gasped and crossed herself. "*Christo…* Mae Maria…"

After much tugging and pushing, the corset finally came together, extruding her figure back to its near pre-pregnant form. Cloirina stepped back to admire herself—her unbridled breasts bulging magnificently under the pressure of the garment. She looked to the maids for approval.

"Well… what do you think?"

"Es shameful," said the older maid.

"Silence! How dare you criticize? I don't want to restrict my milk flow—that is all."

"But you don't feed—"

"Silence! What do you know? You take me for a slut?"

The young maid started to giggle.

"No, Ma'am," said the elder. "Well, perhaps just a little."

Both maids now giggled as they helped her into her revealing dress, Cloirina, all the time, admiring herself in the mirror. "Yes," she said finally, "perhaps a little. Perhaps I need—"

A knock on the door cut her short. "Who is there?"

"It's Michael. I need to speak with you."

Cloirina made an adjustment to her dress, tugging down the bust line. Immediately the old maid attempted to pull it up. "Stop that! I'll finish dressing myself. Let my brother in, then both of you leave. Shoo!"

The maids left as Michael entered. He was shocked to see his sister was still only half-dressed.

"Oh, I'm sorry," he mumbled. "I'll come back when—"

"Come in, little brother," she said with a smile. "You've seen a woman dressing before, haven't you?"

Michael didn't answer; he looked around the room, desperate to find something to occupy his eyes.

"Uncle Walter is not so shy," she said, enjoying the young man's embarrassment. "He watches me all the time. Ask him what he used to do to me when I was your age. It's a family tradition … a truly loving family." Michael stood aghast, unable to speak.

Cloirina continued to study herself in the mirror. "You said you wanted to talk. Has a cat got hold of your tongue? Best speak up; I'm very busy today. Well?"

Michael finally found his voice. "What is to happen?"

"Happen? What do you mean, happen?"

"Maxwell Tunney is here. Will he become *Presidente* of Brazil? Will he take Janus Shar's place? The Americas … is that dead?"

Cloirina angrily turned away from the mirror. "Who told you that? The Americas live! I will see to that. The rest does not concern you."

Michael retreated a few steps. "And what about me?"

Cloirina turned back to the mirror. "If you are worried as to where you feature in the great plan of things, Michael, I have to disappoint you—nowhere!"

The young man was about to protest, but she cut in over him.

"By the time you come of age, it will all be decided. Janus Junior will have it all—that is his destiny."

"But what will become of me?"

"What do you want, little brother?"

"Out! Out of this madness!"

Cloirina stopped fussing with her dress and suddenly pulled him to her, hugging and suffocating him into her huge bosom. "I do love you, Michael," she said softly, "but there has never been time for such luxuries. Whatever you want, name it … anything! Money, favors—"

"Art!" he blurted out, "I want art, something that is totally my own. I'm not a team player. Can I do that? Paris, Madrid, Rome, *Londres*—I just want out!"

"Yes, Michael, you can do that, and I think sooner rather than later. I'm risking all on Maxwell Tunney—and it may bring us all down."

"When?"

"You go as soon as it can be arranged. Now leave me. Have Maxwell Tunney brought to me in the morning room in ten minutes. Speak to him, Michael. Try to get to know him a little."

Michael sighed with relief and hurried out.

III

Cloirina looked devastatingly beautiful. She stood alone in the Jade Palace morning room, her upper and lower body dancing an exotic rumba as she shook the mixer, fixing drinks.

A maid entered and curtsied. "Maxwell Tunney, Tri-President of the United States of America and Canada, Ma'am." Cloirina nodded and the maid left, leaving Max standing agape by the open door as Cloirina upped the shaker's tempo.

She spoke with her back to him. "Maxwell Tunney." She poured two drinks then turned to face him, "That name you would say in the same breath as Janus Shar." She smiled, offering him a glass. "Janus Shar, Maxwell Tunney—the world would quake when it heard those names. So ... hello, Maxwell!"

"Just call me Max," he said as he walked into the room and took the drink. "Thanks." He gulped it down. "It's been a long time. So, what do I call you? Ma'am? Ms. Braganza? Cloirina?"

She smiled. "Call me what you call all your women." She attempted to mimic his gruff voice. *"Hey, bitch!"*

He gave her a look of impatience. "So what do I call you?"

"Why, Cloirina! Same as I was to Janus Shar … just Cloirina. Now for what does Brazil owe this pleasure?"

"I said I'd come. I keep my promises."

"Oh! Are there Americans that don't?"

"Just a figure of speech. Anyways, I'm Canadian … and I wanted to come."

"Then what kept you? It's been over six months."

"What kept me? Protocol kept me. We have a coalition, a tri-presidency; three of us: me, Henning and—"

"Wesley Shar. I know that. Now, what kept you?"

"I couldn't just up and leave." This was not going to plan. He'd meant to be in command, but now found himself making excuses like a cheating husband to a disgruntled wife or mistress. "I have to be around to keep up my claim, for Christ sake?" He raised his voice at the last words, making the statement into a question.

"Oh? Wesley Shar spends most of his time in Alaska, so I'm informed."

He was about to answer, but Cloirina continued. "And don't blaspheme! Did you have a good time in Las Vegas, Mr. Tri-President? How did Vena treat you?"

Max choked on his drink. "Jesus Christ! How in hell do you know about that?"

"And you will not blaspheme in my presence, Maxwell. We may need God on our side. And I do know everything."

"Everything? Then you know why I'm here."

"Everything!" She gave a mocking smile. "And how's BB?"

His face flashed with anger. "What the hell do you mean?"

"Why, how is Janus Shar's widow? Is she well? Has she coped? I know everything, but I still want gossip."

"I don't do gossip, Lady," said Max, bewildered, not knowing whether she knew about the affair or not.

Cloirina studied him for a few moments. She was testing his metal. She looked into his eyes. Max looked back uncomfortably. At length, she smiled and looked away; he'd passed the test—she saw right through him. Max was Max: transparent, nothing more nothing less, what you saw was what you got. She liked that.

"Not many people knew about you and BB. I was cruel about her. I'm ashamed of that."

For a fleeting moment, Max thought about denying it, but he didn't. "BB is a fine woman. And if you know so much, you'll know we only started our—when their divorce was agreed."

"Did you know Janus knew about your affair, Maxwell?"

Max was stunned. "He knew?"

"Oh yes. Janus was a very shrewd man. To please the people, he played us all off. You just played your part—like I played mine."

"Dear God. He knew!"

"So, Maxwell, as I said ... for what does Brazil owe this pleasure?"

"I've come to see you—not just Brazil."

"I'm flattered—liar!"

"Hey!"

"Hey, watch your mouth, bitch!" Cloirina mocked.

Max wanted to come back with something smart, but words failed him. She smiled and continued. "The Americas ... you want to deal."

"Yeah, that's part of it, but mostly I came to see you. Wesley Shar wanted to come, but I insisted."

As she collected his empty glass, she raised an eyebrow. "Insisted? I'm impressed. Why couldn't you have insisted months ago—when I needed a friend? When I was vulnerable? I don't like being vulnerable, Maxwell, not with relatives like mine around."

"Surely you're not at risk from your own family?"

"Oh, Maxwell, how naive you are. You've lived in a country that boasts morals. We cannot afford such luxuries."

She poured him another drink. Max took it without a word and drank it down in a single mouthful. She filled another glass from a decanter.

"Time for whisky, I think. I know your brand."

"Thanks," he said grudgingly, taking the glass.

"I could tell you things about my family that would make you physically sick. I..." She stopped and shook away the notion. "Enough of this ... The Americas. We get the work out of the way—then we play. You'll like the way I play, Maxwell. I saw the way you looked at me at the funeral."

"Max, please. I hate Maxwell."

She smiled. "Max."

He finished his drink and thought a moment. "Okay, you know what I want. Now, what do you want?"

"I hope you are not vegetarian, Max. I've ordered for you Argentine steak, a week hung."

In the magnificent dining room, Max and Cloirina continued their conversation over dinner.

"Brasilia to be Southern Capital … Yes?" Her words echoed around the vast room.

Max was thoughtful for a moment, knowing this was only part of it. "Hmmm, hmm," he said, still chewing. "Good steak." She raised an eyebrow that demanded he answer the question. He continued chewing for a few more moments, and then swallowed. "Sounds reasonable, but remember I can't promise. As I say, I'm just one-third of a trio. Anything else?"

"Shall we take coffee on the veranda?"

The veranda overlooked the city. As evening approached, the distant lights began to dance in the shimmering warm air and sparkle against the sun. Max was mesmerized, lost in thought. Cloirina took away his empty coffee cup and returned with a tray of drinks.

"Yes, there is something else." She poured him a huge scotch. Max raised an eyebrow, shrugged. She handed him his drink and continued. "As founder member of The Americas, I claim dominion over all Southern states." She said it quickly, then looked away to the city lights, and waited.

Max was silent for a moment. "Ow! You don't want much, do you? You'll have a hard time with that. Argentina—"

"Just leave Argentina to me."

Max smiled. "There's something else?"

"Do you think we ought to make love, Maxwell? Would you like that?"

Max smiled again; he'd wondered what had happened to dessert. "Yes, I would like that. It would not be politic to refuse."

Max was better making love than making deals. As he found his way around the great bed with a gentleman's cunning, he thought, *'if world politics were conducted in the bedroom, there'd probably be... a hell of a lot more trouble.'* He conceded and put the stupid notion out of his head.

Cloirina, initiating most of the moves, proved a wonderful, considerate lover. But later, his passion subsided; Max pondered the bespoke 'something else.' He lent across Cloirina's naked body and whispered. "There is something else, Cloirina. Isn't there?"

She pulled the silk sheet over her exposed nakedness and looked Max in the eyes.

"Myself as Regent—answerable to the President— of course."

"Regent? Where in the hell do you think we are … nineteenth-century Britain? This is the modern world."

Cloirina sat up. She let the covering sheet slip away as she spat her words. "You think we're different from them? They lied, fucked, and died just like us. Sex

146

and power, that is all there is, Maxwell. We are no different."

Max rolled his eyes. "Don't swear—it don't suit you." He roughly threw back the silk sheets. "I'm hungry. Show me the kitchen and I'll make us an early breakfast."

In the magnificent kitchen, Max cooked up a huge pile of scrambled egg and crispy bacon. Cloirina left him to it. She had never so much as boiled water in her entire life, whereas Max was as handy in the kitchen as he was in the bedroom. Appetite—and the satisfaction of —was everything to Max.

"So," she said, waiting until they'd finished eating. "What is your answer? What do you think?"

"What do I think? I think you ask too much. What do *you* think?"

She daintily touched her mouth with a crisply starched linen napkin and stood up, seeming to gain superiority as she looked down on him. "Listen, Max, we have unfinished business, you and I. You are one of three. If you concede to all my demands, then they will know that you are the man."

Max looked up at her for a long time without answering. She stared back with demanding eyes. He could feel her mind working—cogs turning, wheels within wheels. "Not a chance in hell," he said at length. "You think I'd give half The Americas away just for a jump in the sack and a hickory-grilled steak? Not a chance in hell!"

Cloirina didn't blink an eye; she'd expected some such reaction. He was, after all, transparent. "Think,

Maxwell, think! I feel the same, as I know you feel. Janus almost did it."

"You're mad! Janus was President. I've yet to be elected."

"No! You were Vice President to Janus Shar—that makes you President, now he's gone. And that's constitutional. The other two are just pretenders ... usurpers."

"I'm President in name only—the Constitution demands an election."

"To hell with the Constitution! Where was your Constitution when they offered Janus an extra term?"

Max picked up his coffee and blew mindlessly into it. Cloirina, suddenly calm, took the cup from his hand.

"Is cold already, Maxwell. Let me fill it." She poured more and handed it back to him.

"Thanks."

"You are President, and, if you give them The Americas, they will give to you what they offered to Janus."

"What? Me? President for life?" He laughed nervously. "I don't think so."

"More than life, Maxwell." She caught hold of his hand and looked into his eyes. "Hereditary!"

"My God—the monarchy again! What's it to be? Queen Cloirina? Ha!" He laughed and started to hum "God Save the Queen." Cloirina flushed. She leapt at him and slapped his face, hard. Max just smiled and continued laughing. She slapped his face again—and again ... a huge slap.

Max grabbed her hand as she attempted to hit him again. He held onto her with one hand and dabbed a little trickle of blood running from his nose with the other. "Damn you," he said as he let her go.

"You will never laugh at me again," she said, rubbing her wrist. "Do you hear? Never!"

He pulled out his handkerchief and wiped away the blood. "Damn you! You're crazy!"

"No, not crazy. Was Janus crazy?"

"Why ask so much? You almost won me over. I could have given you the southern capital—maybe dominion over the rest of the southern states ... worded differently, of course. But... why? Why so much?"

"Because it is there, Maxwell, the old mold is broken. The Republic died with Janus ... when your Senate offered him the extra term. But now it's there for the taking. And if we don't take it, Wesley surly will."

Max was thoughtful for a moment. "You're overlooking Henning."

"Henning-*shlemming*. Forget him. Wesley Shar has."

"You got it all worked out—don't you?"

"Max," she said, approaching with open arms, "it's our destiny." She hugged him and kissed him full on the lips, a long sensual kiss. Max reciprocated, crudely grabbing at her breasts and buttocks. She didn't pull away.

Max finally pushed her away. "Not today, Lady. Nice try, but I ain't buying secondhand goods. Not today."

Cloirina was not shocked. She knew that winning Max over would be no walk-in-the-park. "What about us—The Americas?"

"There is no us. You're too expensive to wear every day of the week. I can't afford you—neither can America. Now, if there's nothing else, I have to leave."

"When you come back, Maxwell … the price—and the prize—will be exactly the same … and you will be back."

Max strode from the room, slamming the door behind him.

IV

It was bitter cold; the weak sun shone like a spotlight behind a curtain of freezing mist. "My God," said Max to his driver and aide as he left his limousine. "Alaska is breathtakingly beautiful."

The aide nodded confirmatively. He and his sentinel companion's dark, sun-shaded eyes did not leave the dash mirror or wing mirror for a second. Both were scrutinizing the road they had just traveled—the answer was mechanical. "Yes, Sir, beautiful, Sir."

Max shook his head despondently, and then made his way alone through the icy snow to the entrance of Wesley Shar's mansion, where Terrence—the late General Pascalo's aide—waited for him in the portico.

"Terry! Good to see you," said Max, blowing into his hands against the cold. "I heard about your new job. Sleeping with the enemy, eh?"

"Sleeping?" gasped Terrence. "I'd sooner eat broccoli!"

"So, how come?"

"I came highly recommended," he answered with a cock of his head. "Wesley's aunt, BB, was second cousin and best*est* friends with Mercedes Pascalo; she put the word in. In return, I keep her informed with gossip. Oh, what a wicked web we weave when first we practice to snitch! Wesley sees it as a regal appointment. I'm his court jester; Touchstone to his Lear."

"Well, you can't keep a good man down—that's what I say."

"Oh, you can," said Terence with an impish smile. "If you're experienced enough—and there's not many around with my experience."

Max smiled back. "You don't mind if I just take your word for that, do you, Terry?"

"Your loss, Mr. Tri-President."

"So, how is your new boss? And don't take all day to tell, I'm freezing out here." Max waited for one of Terence's famed rhetorical answers.

"Wesley Shar, Sir, is—in the words of the immoral Noel Coward—a cunt! You'll excuse my Southern directness, but you did ask. The Anglo-Saxons were visionaries. When they invented that word, they had a Wesley Shar in mind."

Max, shaking with mirth, hurried past Terence into the house.

Terence nimbly overtook him, and led the way inside where he announced him: "Tri-President Maxwell Tunney, Sir."

Wesley Shar, working at his desk, did not look up. Joseph Henning, third member of the constitutional Tri-Presidency, gave a non-committal smile and nod to Max.

Terence, annoyed at being ignored, rolled his eyes at Max. "Shar!" he barked, raising his voice in dramatic pretense, as if Wesley—rather than being officiously rude—had simply not heard him. "It's Maxwell Tunney come to see you, Sir. Isn't that nice?"

Henning smiled again, acknowledging the ruse. Wesley still did not look up.

"He likes to be called, Shar," Terence whispered to Max on his way to the door. "He thinks it sounds like tsar."

"Tsar-een, more like," added Max. They both laughed.

Finally, Wesley looked up. "You two having a good time at my expense?"

Terence shrugged and walked out.

"Hello, Wes," said Max affectionately. "Still as uptight as ever? How you been?"

Wesley stood up and offered his hand. Max grabbed it with two hands.

Wesley gave him a grudging smile. "Good. And you?"

"Yeah, I'm okay."

"And how is Cloirina Braganza, Maxwell?"

"Back-burner—slowly, slowly, catchie monkey."

Henning smiled lewdly. "Did you … you know?"

"Yes," added Wesley. "Did you do the job?"

Max walked over to the desk and smiled conspiratorially to Henning. They shared the comedy of Wesley's naïveté. "No," he said. "I didn't do the job. As I said, back-burner … she wants too much for what she's offering."

Wesley sat back at his desk. As he shuffled his papers, he said, "Perhaps I could do better?"

Max glanced at Henning. He winked and whispered, "Not while there's a hole in your ass." Henning choked off his laughter. Max leaned toward Wesley. "I don't think so, Wes," he said, trying to hide his mirth. "My advice is let her stew."

Wesley, now paying full attention, sat back in his chair and confronted Max. "There's been a … development, Maxwell." He turned to Henning. "Shall I tell him, Joseph, or will you?"

Henning walked a little way from the desk and turned his back on Max. "I'm out of the equation," he said bluntly, and then turned to face him. "I thought it best I do it now—before committing my people's money to a fruitless campaign. My third goes to Wesley."

"The fuck it does! No way!"

"Nothing I can do, Max, I'm stymied … my backers. Sorry."

Max, turning from Henning, glared at Wesley. "I'm still constitutional President. We split it two ways—or I take all."

Wesley stood and walked around the desk to face Max. "That's not an option, Maxwell. It's not a question of seats—it's a question of finance. You couldn't possibly match my proffer."

Max smacked his forehead with the palm of his hand. "My God. Is that what it comes down to? Money?"

"In the end, yes. But there's worse to come—there is still a third contender. Pooley has raised his ugly head. The son, Pooley the younger."

"Pooley? Pooley the goddamn embryo, for Christ's sake! How old is he?"

Henning walked to the door and offered a parting comment. "Old enough, Max—and he's his father's son, all right. A mean-hearted bigot with fire in his belly for revenge." He nodded to Wesley, and then turned back to Max. "Sorry Max. Money, in the end, always talks." He then left. Wesley returned to his desk and continued reading his papers.

Max watched patiently for a moment. He did not enjoy being ignored. He leaned over to Wesley and spoke directly into his face. "I hear Pooley's a goddamn cokehead."

Wesley moved his chair back, regaining his personal space. "That may be, Maxwell, but he's cyber-buying. He's playing conglomerate chess over the global net, tying up Middle and Southern American territories."

"So?"

"So, we can't be seen to be divided, Maxwell, or he'll run right through us. We need to show the world we two are united."

"Then we need to sort out this Henning thing. I want my due, and I ain't—"

"I take it you are, at present, a free agent. I mean, no regular woman—whatever—in the frame?"

"What do you mean, whatever? And what the hell's it to you?"

"My aunt—you and BB?"

Max took a step toward Wesley. "Why, you little skunk. I'll—"

"BB confided in me, Maxwell." Wesley moved behind the shelter of his desk. "She wanted to know how I would take to her marrying her husband's Vice President."

"Max, for God's sake, how many goddamn times I got to tell you? Max!"

Wesley retreated further. "Max!"

"So, it was you that got to her. What did you tell her? Whatever it was, she just up and left."

"She came to me, Max, for advice. She invited me to Blue Haven. She was worried. I wanted none of it. It was she who broached the subject."

Betty Shar had swallowed her pride. The former First Lady took a deep breath and waited, but Wesley was not forthcoming; she had to prompt.

"So, Nephew, what do you think?"

She and Wesley were walking, arm-in-arm, in the magnificent Blue Haven rose garden. Although pale and worried, she still appeared stunningly beautiful in her mourning black. He, white and drawn, was his normal sickly self. She'd never really liked nor understood Wesley—never had the chance to get to know him. But now she needed favor—favor that only he, as head of the family, the money, could grant.

"We must consolidate," he said at length, feigning prudence. "We must show unity. If this were France or Italy or even England ... who knows?"

"Then we'll live in France or Italy or even England."

"Think this out to its conclusion. I don't want to be an overbearing influence, but I must point out the terms of Janus's will."

"We shan't marry, if that's what's worrying you."

"Worrying me? Please, Aunt, don't get this wrong. It is not I that objects. Janus Shar's reputation is already tainted by Cloirina Braganza. If this party is to go forward to the next presidency, there must be much bridge building. If you two were to live together—here or even abroad—the paparazzi would have a field day. You would be their new Diana. And what would you live on? There is the clause in the will—"

"You wouldn't—"

"It wouldn't be up to me."

"But you wouldn't block my claim?"

Wesley remained silent. BB's eyes filled with tears. Without further word, she turned and walked off alone, toward the house.

Max studied Wesley. He knew him as immoral, scheming, and unscrupulous—but never as a liar.

"I didn't have to tell her, Max," said Wesley, trying to sound sympathetic. "She already knew."

For a moment, Wesley thought Max would strike him. Max's face went through a series of changes— from murderous fury to blind anger—finally settling on cold realization. Wesley would live to fight another day. "So, Max," he said with relief. "No woman." He chanced a smile. "I understand you once had a thing … with my sister?"

Max looked at him in disbelief. "A thing? What the hell do you mean—a thing?"

"Geraldine always liked you—God knows why. We, the family, decided to try to turn her off you. We all thanked God you beat us to it."

"What the hell are you driving at?"

"I'm driving at unity—multi-billion dollar unity."

"You trying to sell me your sister, Wesley? Pimping is a tad out of your line, wouldn't you say so?"

"No, I would not say so. When the time comes, I too will have to make a marriage. Old time religion, old time marriage. We all have to make sacrifices, Maxwell."

"Sacrifices!" Max spat the word into Wesley's face. "Whoever marries you will make the ultimate sacrifice, you limp-wristed, fucking pervert."

"One day, Maxwell, you will regret saying these things. You never miss an opportunity to put me down. I used to think of you as family. You never liked me … nobody likes me."

Max sighed and slapped his arm around the dejected man's shoulders. Max knew the misery Wesley had suffered as a child—he was not of the same stuff as the rest of the Shar family. When they eventually became aware of his sexuality, he was all but shunned. "You're so wrong, kid. I always liked you. I told you that as many times as I could because I thought you needed to know that someone cared. And you're not unlikeable, but goddamn it, you make it difficult sometimes"

"You have no idea—"

"Yes, I do. I know exactly what it was like for you as a kid … what they expected and how disappointed they all were … about what you are … what you became."

"Homosexual. Say it, Max! You've called me all the other names. Yes, homosexual—and I will still make the sacrifice and conventionally marry. Mormons don't take too well to gay marriages."

Max knew Wesley was right—they all had to make sacrifices. BB was to be his. He looked toward the door, wishing he were the other side of it, "So ... what have you got in your twisted little mind for me?"

Wesley leaned on his desk. He spoke to the back of Max's head. "Think what's at stake, Maxwell. If Pooley gets the big job—and he could—we can kiss The Americas good-bye, because he won't want to be seen picking up Janus Shar's brainchild."

V

Truman P. Pooley Jr. stood alone, staring in the mirror of the plush bathroom at his campaign headquarters. He ran his fingers through his greased-back hair, contemplating his youthful image. After a few moments, an aide entered.

"Did you get it?" Pooley said without looking away from his reflection.

"Yeah. I got it." The aide took a package from his pocket and offered it.

"Don't fucking hand it to me, jerk! I don't want my dabs on it. Make me two good lines ... here, along on the ledge, then flush the rest away. And don't ever carry stuff on you. When I want more, you go get more, okay?"

The aide made the two lines of white powder on the ledge in front of Pooley, and then flushed the rest of the package into a toilet.

"And I didn't hear you answer, jerk-off. Don't you ever ignore me."

"Okay, I heard you … sorry. It's just that I don't like doing this. I don't think you should—"

"Where the fuck do you get off, boy? Do I look like I give a fuck what you think? I spent a zillion bucks today. Bought a goddamn state, near on. You any idea what that feels like?"

The aide had contempt in his eyes as he answered. "No, I don't believe I do."

"Well, it sure beats the hell out of sucking dick, I can tell you that, cocksucker! So don't you ever ignore me, right?"

Pooley snorted the two lines. Immediately the drug bit in. He twitched a couple of times and then rubbed the residue onto his teeth. He looked back into the mirror and wiped his nose, then stared at the aide for a few seconds. "I said, right?"

The aide jolted to attention. "Sure, I just meant—"

"Fuck! There you go again! I don't care what goes on in that sphincter fucking brain of yours. You're just a pair of legs to me … fetching and carrying. Now beat it. And keep in earshot. Go on, go, go!"

The aide flushed with anger and walked out without another word. Pooley shrugged and studied his reflection again. He smiled adoringly at himself as he adjusted his nose with a couple of sideways twitches.

When he entered the boardroom, there was no trace of the smile. He surveyed the dozen or so male executives sitting around the huge oak table. At length, he sat at the head. Immediately the room pricked up its ears, ready and eager to toady and hang onto his every word—except for one brashly dressed young man who fiddled continuously with a tiny computer game.

"Okay, team," Pooley announced, still rubbing at his nostrils. "No more easy riding ... the boy from Brazil is back in town ... Tunney. Watch him, he's twice them other two cocksuckers stuck together."

A huge, fat man attempted to speak.

"Excuse me—"

"I'm still fucking talking!" Pooley exploded over him. "Don't ever interrupt me, Felix. You know nothing I wanna hear. If you did know something, it would be because I'd have said it fucking first."

Felix Churchwood, an inoffensive man in his middle fifties offered a silent apology and looked to the rest of the group for support. All avoided eye contact. He shrugged and sat back in his seat.

Pooley shook his head in wonderment. "Fucking nerve! Now, when my father—God rest his troubled soul—was in power, he didn't give a shit for this Americas charade. That's why them scum-sucking, greaseball Latino bastards killed him. But believe me—they will pay. Oh yeah, every last fucking one of them."

Felix, still smarting, started to fidget.

Pooley turned on him. "Goddamn it, keep that fat ass still! You wanna do something useful? Go get me some ice cream ... plain vanilla. Go. Go!"

Felix gave a contemptuous stare and obediently left the room.

Pooley watched him go. "Fucking nerve of that guy, interrupting *me*. Where was I? Oh, yeah ... what's Tunney got to offer: The Americas?" He stopped, and then studied the faces of his executive committee. All looked blankly back at him, unsure if they were expected to answer or not. He shook his head in dismay and continued. "The skunk didn't even have the good manners to be born in America. His presidency is in direct contradiction to our Constitution. As you know, I've made a case to the Senate that he, being Canadian-born, should be stripped of office and an election held immediately." Again he stared at them, one to the other, as if waiting. They twisted awkwardly in their seats, hoping that someone else would say something to move the conference onward.

"Well? What do you think? Christ! Have I got to do all the thinking around here? What do I pay you fucking plankton for?"

They looked at each other nervously, each one considering whether to speak or not. Pooley waved away the notion. He turned to the youngest member, still playing with the computer game. "What do you think, Rook? Tunney?"

Without looking up from his GameBoy, Rook answered in a whining, New England accent. "Tunney is, I construe, no better than he ought to be ... somewhat loftier than his current stature might deem reasonable. As to what the man has to proffer, it seems to me, at this juncture in time, to be about as broad as its constituent parameters might dictate." Rook, content with his offering, continued with his computer game, leaving his bizarre statement hanging.

Pooley studied each man for a reaction ... nothing, no one. His gaze returned to Rook. "My sentiments, boy, exactly."

Embarrassed silence ensued, except for the continual bleeping of the computer game. Mercifully, the door opened and Felix walked back in with a dish of ice cream. Without a word, he placed it in front of Pooley and then took his seat.

Pooley immediately started to eat, noisily and quickly, speaking through mouthful after mouthful. "So. There's to be no election … Tunney wins the day … Money seeming to talk louder than the law. Why am I not surprised? Wesley Shar's money."

He finished the ice cream. "Jesus," he said, scraping the dish and wiping his mouth on the back of his hand. "That was good." He pushed the dish away and continued. "Even now, they're spin-doctoring some cockamamie new deal." There was a mutual shaking of heads. "And I've heard there's a wedding in the offing, Tunney and Shar … sounds like Sonny and Cher. 'I Got You Babe'! Ha! No, not Wesley … not unless Max has taken to humping mud-cake. No, I mean Wesley's tramp sister." Conspiratorial laughter came from everyone except Rook. "But whatever it is, it ain't cutting the mustard with me, and I don't think it will for the American public. And it sure as hell won't with a certain Brazilian whore—if I may call her that." This was greeted with howls of laughter from everyone, again with the exception of Rook. "Okay. Go, go, and be fruitful. Buy, buy, buy! I want one-third of every goddamn country south of the canal. If Tunney does get The Americas, he'll have to pay me fucking rent. I'll call the tune, and whatever the outcome, I will do well … extremely well." He frowned at them and the laughter stopped. "Well? Fuck off! Go, go, go!"

One by one, they stood and left, all except Rook. Across the table, Pooley lowered his head into his folded arms. After a moment, he raised an eye to Rook. "You got a problem, boy?"

"No, *you* got a problem."

"No *problemo*. Just make them fuckers pay … top dollar. It's the only thing that hurts them. Money is the K-Y Jelly of revenge. They have to pay … for my father."

"What about power?"

"Money is power, jerk-off. Don't you know that?"

"Well, I have it in my power to rid you of all three of them. I have infiltrated their campaign data—there are, shall we say, anomalies! Just say the word—and *squat!*" He waved the little computer, and then ran it across his throat.

Pooley studied Rook for a moment. "Me say the word? Why? Why do I have to sanction every goddamn thing? You people don't never learn, do you? There's only ever been one President to lose his job—and that was because he had to shove his tongue up everyone's ass to taste what they had for breakfast."

Rook shrugged and looked back at his computer.

"Now that you've said it out loud, you've fucking implicated me. Either you're wired or this fucking room is wired or there's some goddamn spook across the block with a hyper-mic trained on this room. You should have just done it. Now get the hell out."

Rook shrugged. "Okay. And don't worry, I won't offer again."

"Do I look like I'm fucking worried?"

Rook didn't answer; he just turned and walked out. Pooley watched him go then ruefully sank back into his folded arms.

VI

The white convertible parked precariously in the Washington DC, lover's-lane beauty spot. The lights of the capitol it overlooked sparkled just marginally brighter than the night stars. The driver and his passenger immediately locked together in passionate necking. When they finally pulled apart, the beautiful young woman, Geraldine Shar, hesitantly spoke:

"It ... it won't make any difference, Harry," she whispered. "No matter what your father can do, I have to go along with it ... I just have to."

The young man angrily punched at the steering wheel in tantrum. "It's obscene. That bastard's as old as my father. You can't do it! How you gonna feel with his clammy mitts all over you?" He looked at her, but she looked away. He took her chin and turned her to face him. "Look, we could always—"

"We could always what?" she said, pulling away. "Harry, Harry, if we ran off, what would we do? What could we do ... start a chain of restaurants? Make a zillion bucks in a year like your grandfather did a century ago?" She shook her head as she smiled at him. "We're just the proverbial poor little rich kids ... it'd kill us. And Max Tunney is only twenty years older than me, and he don't have no clammy mitts."

"How about I make you pregnant?"

"How about I bust you in your nose?" She laughed again. "Pregnant. You already did that once. You nearly died of fright."

"What the hell you laughing at? This is serious stuff. Goddamn it! I love you!"

"Yeah ... I know it. It'll only be for convenience, Darling, nothing more. Max Tunney has his eyes elsewhere. He's not an unreasonable guy."

"I heard you dated him already."

"That was a long, long time ago, Harry. When I was really young."

"Did he—"

"To hell with you. No way I'm telling you stuff like that."

"So he did, then?"

She smiled a secret smile. "Look, I'm a Shar. I had my national duties—just like the rest of them."

"So he did then."

Again she ignored the insinuation. "It works like this, Harry: Max was being groomed. He had to be seen about, shall we say, Tinsel town—I was the tinsel. You know, the right places, the right people. It was my national duty. A dirty, filthy job, but ... I did it."

"You bitch. Do you know what this is doing to me?"

Geraldine thought for a moment, then screwed her hands into fists and wrung them in anguish. "You're tearing me apart!" she screamed.

"What the hell?"

"James Dean," she said calmly. "*Rebel Without a Cause*. Move on, Harry, there'll be time for us. You do college—I do Max Tunney. When we both graduate, then it'll be our time ... two years max." She thought for a moment then gave a sudden chuckle. "Get it? Two years, Max. Ha!"

Harry looked at her in amazement, "Christ. In another life, you was a goddamn hooker!"

She shrugged. "So?"

Cloirina stared unblinking into the CCT monitor. From the privacy of her opulent bedroom, she watched her uncle, President Walter Braganza, addressing a hostile Brazilian Senate. The angry assembly jeered and catcalled as the old man tried to speak.

"There is no hidden agenda—none! What you see is what you get—"

"That is Janus Shar talking," an irate Senator called out. "Was he to be the trump card in Cloirina's hand—or should I say in her belly?"

"That's not true!" Walter yelled. "And that is libelous. See? I make a note of your name."

"Make your note!" taunted the Senator. "You don't know what's going on any more than we do. It's her! She is selling this country to America! We demand to know what's going on!" He turned in his seat to take applause from his supporters, and waved a gracious hand.

Walter glared. "Demand? You demand from me? You know what is keeping this economy afloat? US money! The Yankee dollar! Ride in your big shiny American cars—a mile in any direction—you'll see what lies beyond: cardboard cities, poverty … for all of us. Our people, long ago, joined the third-world club. Brazil is kept alive with American money. We have nothing left to sell!" The Senate was quiet. Walter had hit a true note.

From her bedroom, Cloirina switched off the closed-circuit TV, curled up in the sumptuous bed, and pulled the covers over her head.

In the White House gala ballroom, the mood was different. Hermann and Onis, farcically dressed in tuxedos and accompanied by two elegant women, stood among the political and show business dignitaries. They watched Max smooch across the dance floor with Geraldine Shar.

Hermann shook his head in sympathy. "Jesus, just look at the poor sucker. I know what he's wishing tonight."

"Yeah," said Onis. "Wishing he was in Scotland, fishing tonight."

"What?"

"It's a line from *Camelot*, jackass." Onis scrutinized his bemused partner. "The musical? Jesus!"

"What in the hell you jabbering on about, boy?" yapped Hermann, still not understanding. "You need to drink some whisky, quick! You sound like one of Wesley Shar's goddamn faggot buddies."

Onis looked at his partner. "I bet you ain't never been to a theater in your whole life, have you?"

One of the women, in earshot, chipped in. "He has, too. He took me to see *Don Giovanni*." She smiled back at Hermann. "That's right, isn't it, Honey?" She leaned close to Onis and whispered, "The jerk thought Don Giovanni was a stand-up comedian."

"Hey, I heard that!" said Hermann, "and it's a damn lie! I thought it was an Italian restaurant!" He laughed and started to sing, "Don Giovanni, Don Giovanni!"

Onis now joined in. The two men locked arms and sang in unison over the dance band, "Don Giovanni! Don Giovanni! Don Giovanni!"

Max, dancing with Geraldine across the hall, heard them and gave a chastising shake of the head to his riotous boys. They took no notice and continued.

Wesley Shar and Henning were also watching the spectacle. Henning smiled. "I see Tunney's brought along his two tame orangutans."

Wesley shrugged, trying to ignore the loutish spectacle. "I have an angle."

"Yeah? Whatever your angle, you still got to fight him in the ballot box."

"Maybe not. See how good those two look together? If I can seed this marriage, I'll have him."

"How come?"

"Geraldine is a lovely girl, Joe, but she won't be enough for Maxwell Tunney. The people love him as the rascal lover, but they won't stand for adultery. And I know where this dog likes to bury his bone."

"Jesus Christ, Wes. She's your sister! What in hell you getting her into?"

"Politics, my friend ... politics."

Across the ballroom Max—cheek-to-cheek with Geraldine—forced a smile. She feigned something similar and then slipped back to her look of utter boredom.

VII

The procured, whirlwind courtship and subsequent State wedding over, Geraldine stood naked before her husband, rigid like some tailor's dummy. Max, fully dressed, sat immobile on the exquisite king-sized bed. She stood inert, her eyes focused to infinity as he studied her slender body, following every angle and curve of her beauty with undemanding eyes. In spite of his infamous reputation as a ladies' man and rake, Max was no lecher. He knew what was in Geraldine's heart; he saw past her manufactured, seductive smile to the sadness her eyes couldn't hide.

"Married!" Half a continent away, Cloirina's black eyes were wide in rage as she screamed at Max. Alone in the morning room of the Jade Palace, they stared at each other, nose-to-nose. Max fidgeted nervously like a schoolboy on report.

"It's no more than political bonding," he offered, attempting to regain some dignity. "I had to keep my options open."

"And she had to keep her legs open!"

"For God's sake!"

"Don't you dare bring God into this."

Max rolled his eyes, "Look, young Pooley is railroading Shar—and Shar is railroading everybody else. He's swallowed Henning already ... I had to ... political bonding."

"Don't give me 'had to.' Nobody has to, certainly not a president. Did you enjoy her? Was she as good as me?"

"This was business, goddamn it!"

"I know the way it works, Maxwell, you would have had to consummate—convention would have demanded that. Was she a good hump? Is the honeymoon over, or have you got to hurry back?"

"There is no honeymoon. She's with her lover in Costa Rica. I flew directly here—I made a mistake—I'm *never* going back." Max looked away and squeezed his eyes closed. He was momentarily back there, back on his farcical wedding night. He, sitting fully clothed on the bed holding the naked Geraldine, who stood passively in front of him while he caressed every curve of her body like a sculptor contemplating his work. Then, looking up at her with remorseful eyes, whispers, "I'm sorry. You are very beautiful—and I'm sure you would make a wonderful partner. But... sorry." He had given a paternal, farewell kiss on her cheek then walked from the room.

"Bastard!" Cloirina hurled the word, forcing Max to open his eyes.

"Christ, I don't need this. We didn't … I told you; she has a lover … She was forced into it—same as me. We didn't."

Cloirina gave a disbelieving look. "You didn't? I thought you men don't give a damn who you stuck into … any porthole in any storm."

"Yeah, well I didn't. And it's 'any *port* in a storm.'"

"Any port, fucking hole! You have a beautiful … well, pretty young wife … and you didn't—"

"No! So damn well sue me!"

"No … we sue them! Unconsummated! We have the marriage annulled."

"What? No way. Not in America."

"Maybe not in America, but we could in The Americas—and we are in Brazil. Here we have it annulled—the Vatican will agree." She smiled wickedly. "Believe me, Maxwell, they will agree."

"And—"

"We marry."

"And—"

"You concede to all my requests for unification. And demand life presidency from the Latin states for taking them into The Americas."

Max stared, aghast. Was he really having this discussion, this conspiracy, this treason? "Shar won't accept that. That, Lady, is insurrection!"

"No. It's legal. And stop calling him Shar! There was only one Shar—and he is dead! You mean that weasel, Wesley. *You* will be Shar … Shar of all The Americas."

"Legal?"

"Yes, legal. You have the Constitution on your side. You are the rightful President, and the title, President for life, was created legally and offered to Janus Shar, that set the precedent. You are asking no more than what they themselves have already decreed."

Max grabbed her angrily. "You're talking goddamn Civil War!"

"If that's what it takes." She pulled away.

"You know how many Americans died in the last civil war? More than in both World Wars! Father fighting son—brother fighting brother!"

"If that's what it takes!"

Max slapped her hard across the face, sending her reeling. "You murderous bitch!"

She fell in a heap across the room. After a moment, she gathered herself and looked up at him. "Not a civil war, Maxwell—a Holy War: Catholicism against Protestantism, the oldest fight in Christendom. That is why the Vatican will annul the marriage, because they have long, spiteful memories. Think of the Martin Luther/Henry Tudor debacle. They will allow us to marry with the Holy Father's blessing."

Her mouth was bleeding; Max ran to her and lifted her up. "Dear God. I'm so sorry."

She pulled away and continued as if nothing had happened. "We align The Americas with the Holy Catholic Church—divide and conquer. Everybody, even God, has an angle."

Max looked at her. How could he have hit her? He agonized for a few moments before the magnitude of her stratagem began to crystallize.

"Max, it's destiny," she whispered, sensing that she was winning him over. "Our destiny—yours, mine, and Janus Junior. He will inherit?" She stared at him as the plan she had kindled, shuddered through his mind: It was a mad thing, insane, unthinkable … un-American.

"Okay!" said Max. He had made his decision, calm and resolute. "We do it."

Cloirina was still staring at him. "Well…?" he said beginning to feel uneasy. "What? That's what you want, isn't it?"

She turned and walked away—and for the first time touched her face where he'd hit her. "Oh, by the way," she said turning back, "you need to become Catholic." She delivered the statement as an afterthought, almost a throwaway. "And, of course, my son will inherit. Yes?"

He looked back at her with utter surrender, grabbed her, and kissed her blood-smudged mouth.

VIII

The black limousine meandered the mile-long drive to Wesley Shar's Alaskan residence. Rook sat in the rear seat, zombied to his GameBoy, a pigmy to a giant. Only the sight of Wesley's private jet on the adjacent runway momentarily dragged his eye from the lure of the tiny screen.

Wesley Shar strode through the Versailles-worthy gardens to greet the young man. Rook shook his outstretched hand affectedly, first taking the sweat-sticky computer from his fingers. The pair walked off, crunching along the snow-covered path, Wesley's arm firmly around Rook's shoulders.

Hours later, in the crystal-clear moonlight, Wesley Shar caressed Rook's naked body on his king-size, four-poster bed. The GameBoy was idle on the bedside table. Rook was engaged in a different game.

The chapel bells of Santa Maria Cathedral rang out as Max twiddled his thumbs in the nave. Next to him, Cloirina smiled radiantly.

"So, Catholic boy. How does it feel?"

"I feel I could walk on water."

"That just cost you four Hail Mary's."

"I'd do anything for you. God won't be offended, will he? For, you know, my clandestine motive and all?"

"Nothing is clandestine to God, Maxwell. Anyway, he'd better not be offended ... that man owes me."

"God owes you?"

Cloirina turned away. She was about to reveal a dark secret and couldn't bear to see the hurt that she knew it would cause. "Yes, he owes me. When I was a child, life was beautiful. I was beautiful, then—"

"And modest, too?"

"Shut up and listen." She indicated her curvaceous body. "Then these ... things happened to me, and I wasn't beautiful anymore ... I was desirable." She forced herself to turn and look at him. "I tell you this, Darling, because I don't want secrets between us ... not ever." Tears welled in her eyes as she forced herself to continue. "At the age of fifteen, my life suddenly changed. I was a late developer; I knew nothing of sex. Walter Braganza seduced me. God owes me."

Max was shocked, then sickened. "That goddamn degenerate! I'll kill him, I'll—"

"No. It was inevitable. In those days, we lived really close ... for security. Until I was eighteen, I'd never met another boy outside my family. It was inevitable." Max was silent. Cloirina closed her tear-flooded eyes and remembered herself as a young girl in the Jade Palace garden playing tennis with Walter Braganza.

"In his defense," she continued, "Walter was gentle. He wooed me like I was a princess. I was a princess. Walter was the only parent I knew—I hardly ever saw my mother and father."

Her eyes still closed. She now saw her father, President Edmundo Braganza, addressing an adoring crowd from the Jade Palace balcony—now addressing the Senate—and now dancing with his beautiful wife, Rosetta, at a magnificent ball.

"After my parents died, Walter became my guardian." She now pictured Edmundo and Rosetta Braganza on their fatal ride into Argentina—the limousine engulfing in flames, followed by a deafening explosion.

Cloirina opened her eyes and the images were gone.

"As I say, it was inevitable."

Max's face was dark with anger. "No, that wasn't inevitable. My breaking his fucking, skinny, scrawny neck—that is inevitable!"

"Maxwell, remember where you are … four more Hail Mary's. Now, let me finish, I want you to know all."

She closed her eyes again and was immediately transported back to the Jade Palace: Walter making love to her; stripping her and she, dancing naked in the grand ballroom. "He did everything to me, Max, everything, except actually …"

She saw in her mind's eye, as voyeur, the memories she'd long put away. She watched as she continued the commentary on her own tender seduction. "You see, I was to make a good, Catholic bride—Uncle Walter was very careful not to … spoil me. He needed me because he was steadily working his way through our family fortune. I had to make a good marriage … money, money, money. When I went to my wedding bed I was a virgin … *virgo*, unimpeachably *intacto*."

"He raped you?"

"No, I just told you—he seduced me."

"We call that statutory rape—*rape* by any other name. Did you … enjoy it?"

"I am human—that is all I have to say on that."

She stood up and walked a couple of steps away from him, then looked back to the great altar. She saw the image of herself in an exquisite white gown, marrying an ugly old man. She quickly opened her eyes, not wanting to see more.

Max looked into her eyes then looked away. "So, what happened to your husband?"

"I killed him," she said without emotion.

"*What!* How, for Christ's sake?"

"With love. Four more Hail Mary's, better watch your tongue. I loved him to death. Three months … his heart."

Max forced a sardonic smile. "Lucky old stoat."

"And I inherited half of Brazil."

"Worth every penny." He grabbed her around the waist and tugged her to him.

She gave him a damning look and pulled away. "You may think me mercenary, Maxwell, but I thought the world of that old man. He was kind and loving—and he was my friend. I have no regrets."

"I'm sorry, Honey, I really am. I didn't mean—"

"No need to be sorry. I just wanted you to know that that was everything. No secrets?"

"Did you love Janus?"

"Why, yes. Yes!"

"More than me?"

She looked at him and laughed, mimicking his voice. "Would I love the moon more than the sun? I have only known old men, Maxwell. You ... you are my toy-boy."

"Don't fuck with me, you hear? I've put my life on the line for you, Lady. Who would you sooner it be—him or me?"

"Hey, bitch!" she growled, again mimicking his gruff voice.

"Yeah ... bitch!"

"Don't give me that little-boy-lost look. You know ... you know without my saying. You've never had a single doubt since you saw me smile at you at the funeral, have you? Have you?"

Max smiled back. "Not a single one. Bitch."

"You are the love of my life, Maxwell Tunney ... for the rest of my life."

He took her in his arms again. "Me, too." His voice was tender now. "If I had just one day left on Earth and I could spend it with you, I'd think myself a goddamn lucky guy." He started to caress her, but she pulled away.

"You've no time for this ... four more Hail Mary's, Darling. You are going to be a busy Catholic boy."

Max crossed himself, smiled, and tried to kiss her. Again, she turned away, laughing. He pursued her and pulled her into a long kiss.

IX

Wesley Shar stood at a lectern, attempting to manufacture a face of unyielding disgust. He was again addressing the Senate.

"Yes Senators, for life, and it's constitutional. When you, the Senate, so graciously afforded that privilege to my uncle, Janus Shar, it automatically fell, on his demise, to his Vice President. Which, ladies and gentlemen, means he doesn't need to be reelected."

This was greeted with gasps of disbelief from the packed ranks.

A matronly Senator stood and hurled her words. "The hell he does! We created that amendment—now we revoke it. —Ontario."

Wesley turned on her with contempt. "Just like that, Ontario?"

"Yes, Mr. President, just like that."

"You think it's that simple?"

"Simple or not ..."

Wesley gave an undetected smile of triumph. Things were going as he had anticipated. "In his declaration," he continued, "of the UNSA ..." He paused, knowing they were unfamiliar with the term. "... The Unified Nations of Southern America, Maxwell Tunney offered the USA and Canada the opportunity to join in creating The Americas. If we take it up, we take Tunney up, as life President, and his new wife as First Lady." These words echoed around the Senate hall to stunned, utter silence.

Half a continent away, Cloirina and Max were exchanging marriage vows in a magnificent state wedding.

After Cloirina arrived the customary twenty minutes late, the ceremony went off without a hitch—except for Max clumsily dropping the wedding ring on the point of exchanging—the gold band echoing around the chapel as it clattered across the marble floor, drawing shocked 'oohs' and 'ahhs' from the guests.

After the wedding—blessed and solemnized in the highest Catholic tradition—the happy couple exited the cathedral to a multitude of cheering, flag-waving spectators who crammed the streets all the way to the Jade Palace. At the celebration parties, people drank beer and caipirinhas. Music was everywhere. Little parties started down every side street; every fifty yards was a party with loud-speakers piled up or a hi-fi cradled on a shoulder, people dancing, throwing streamers, and spraying silly-string. Wherever music started, a crowd would miraculously appear, drinking and dancing and throwing confetti over themselves and everyone. When Cloirina had thrown her bouquet into the crowd, the cheering had reached fever pitch, to which even an invasion of the pitch at a World Series or World Cup Soccer Final could not have equaled.

When Max arrived at the palace, he led his new bride into the portico. He picked her up and carried her over the threshold through a shower of gold and silver streamers.

The grim mood of the Senate had finally found its voice; their gasps and groans gave an inward elation to Wesley's outward anger. "Yes, wife! So now add bigamy to his list. Yes, Texas?"

The Senator for Texas stood and cleared his throat. "The Americas: we must negotiate. It's too important to turn our backs on just because of a family feud. I say keep negotiations open. We keep Tunney in the tent because there's nowhere else for him to piss—except over us. —Texas."

"You, of all people, should tread carefully, Senator. You have greedy neighbors now. I have it on good authority that Panama is just about in Tunney's pocket— and when that happens, Nicaragua will follow, then Mexico. How do like them apples, Texas?"

The Senator answered from his seat. "He can't take Mexico. That state is mortgaged up to its eyeballs— trillions. And you yourself better tread carefully; I have it on good authority that Pooley now owns half of Alaska."

"I think not, Texas. Pooley is out of the running … permanently! As we speak, that degenerate sits sniffing and adjusting his nose in a Washington DC, jail! I can tell you now—it will be common knowledge tomorrow—Pooley is to face charges of corruption, insider-trading, and Mafia-linked fraud! And that's on *my* authority."

The whole House registered shock. Wesley continued over the animated chatter. "There are, however, foreign buyers. We have old enemies with long memories, it would seem."

Wesley knew he had them. One more twist of the knife and they would give him what he wanted. "When Maxwell Tunney has Middle America, he will have control of the canal!" He paused to ensure they comprehended the full implication. "And, if we refuse his offer, he intends to deny access to all US shipping until we capitulate! A siege, gentlemen—a new Suez Crisis—this time in Panama!"

A lone Senator stood and waited with a grave expression on his gnarled face.

Wesley indicated toward him. "What do you have to say to that, Idaho?"

"I say if he so much as stops one goddamn US ship, it's—"

"It's what, Senator? *War?* Max Tunney has the ninth fleet under Admiral Keating—half in the Pacific Ocean and half in the Caribbean Sea."

Now, among the nervous mumbling, another Senator stood and hurled his words, "How, in God's name, was he allowed to do that? —Flo'da."

"How, Florida? Why? Because Max Tunney is still President of these United States—that's how!" Wesley smashed his fist on the lectern. "I demand this House declare a state of emergency—immediately!"

He watched their faces as the words sank in. "And, in retaliation, as a show of force, I intend to redeploy the Gulf fleet. And in retaliation, as a show of force, I intend to impeach Tunney in his absence! Furthermore …" he paused again, as if his words were drowned out—draining every last drop of drama.

The Senator for Florida stood for a second time and shouted over the din, urging Wesley to continue. And... "*And...?* What else you got up your sleeve? —Flo'da."

Wesley eyed the Senator until he was forced to look away. "Furthermore… by default, as the only surviving member of the lawful Tri-Presidency, I declare myself *sole* President." The cheering changed to gasps of shock. "Sole acting President, that is … until the state of emergency is over. Then, God willing, we return to normality: Presidential nominations and constitutional election."

The house was still silent, save for a few intense mumblings. Wesley surveyed them, committing the dissenters to memory—and of these, there were many. He knew that he wasn't liked, but he also knew he was leaving them little room for maneuver.

"Gentlemen, we are entering our darkest, most dangerous hours. Never before has this country's territory been under threat of invasion. Not even the Cuban missile crisis threatened that. Yes, Texas."

Texas stood, turned from Wesley to hurl his words at his fellow Senators. "He's right! What in hell are y'all waiting for? —Texas."

Wesley smiled at his lone vocal supporter. "In our hour of need, we cannot be seen to be divided. We cannot be seen to be without a President. I beg you, put away your petty arguments, put them aside and unite now—before it's too late."

Texas stood again. "He's right! You haven't got the bastard snapping at your heels. I go along with that—sole President until the end of the state emergency." He snapped a military salute to Wesley, and then sat.

Wesley folded his arms and swept his gaze from one side of the house to the other. "If there is any opposition, let us hear it now."

"We're right behind you, Shar," yelled Texas, then again turned in his seat to address the whole house. "The hell you people waiting for—a goddamn invasion? Come on, three cheers for President Shar. Hip, hip—Hoorah!" Just a few of the Senators responded. Texas shouted again, "Hip, hip—Hoorah!" This time, fully half responded. He shouted even louder, stood and beckoned with his arms to encourage them. "Hip, hip—hoorah!" All the Senators now responded, cheering wildly. A chanting commenced, and was quickly picked up by the entire house. "Shar! Shar! Shar! Shar!"

Wesley let the chanting continue. Eventually he brought the house to an unruly order. "I take that as a positive." The cheering only subsided after he'd held up his hands for a full minute. "Thank you, thank you! My only regret is that my first task as sole President is to inform this noble house that this great country of ours is technically at war!" More applause signified that his first Presidential declaration had been unanimously accepted.

As the cheering subsided, Florida stood again. "That's all very cozy, but the fleet will need a week at least to make the Canal Zone. What does Mr. *Sole* President intend to do in the interim? —Flo'da."

Wesley pulled himself to his full height, "Interim? There is no interim … it's done, Mr. Faint-Heart Florida—done! I wasn't about to wait for no goddamn blockade, my war task force has already slipped anchor!" Thunderous cheering erupted. "Our gulf forces are just twenty-four short hours from the Caribbean … and it's going through the canal come hell or high water!"

Riotous whooping and cheering erupted, to which Wesley raised a clenched fist, accepting their adoration. He smiled and turned aside. "I'm learning, Uncle Max. I'm learning."

"Give him to me," snapped Cloirina as she entered the magnificent nursery. "I will hold little JJ."

The nurse looked surprised and turned the child away protectively. "Is not ready, Ma'am." After a moment of thought, she added, "You are not used to holding him."

Cloirina thrust out her arms toward the baby, "Give him to me—now!" She grabbed the child out of the woman's hands.

"*Christo*, Maria! Don't hold him like that. Please be careful. He jumps. He—"

"Do not tell me to be careful with my own child! You think I don't know how to be a mother?"

"No, Ma'am… I mean, yes, Ma'am. Just that he has started to—how you say—wiggle."

"Of course he wiggles; he's nearly six months old. He is a Shar! He will be walking soon."

The nurse hovered as Cloirina rocked the baby clumsily in her arms. "You don't normally want to—"

"What? What? I don't normally want to what … hold him? What do you know? I always want to hold him. It's just I'm too busy."

Max now entered. He was pleasantly surprised to see Cloirina holding the child. "My God—you two look so sweet together."

Cloirina smiled back at him, acting the doting mother. "I hold him all the time. These nurses are far too clumsy … they don't have the motherly touch." She looked at the nurse and flicked her head. "You may go. Go on, shoo!"

The nurse looked daggers back and poked out her tongue. Cloirina did likewise, and then smiled an impish smile. The nurse cocked her head and walked out.

Max crossed the room and kissed Cloirina's cheek. "So, how is little JJ today?"

"He's fine—he said his first words today."

"Oh, really? And what did he say?"

Cloirina whispered to the child, "Tell Papa what you said, little JJ." She then provided the baby's answer. "What you see, Papa, is what you get."

Max smiled. "He said all that?"

"Oh, yes—and lots more. He talks all the time to me. You do love him, Max … Janus Shar's son … you do love him?"

Max took the child from her arms and held him aloft. "Love this ugly, smelly bunch of rags?"

"Not rags—a smelly bunch of silk."

"You betcha I love him. I loved Janus—and I love Janus Junior … he's my son now."

"And did you love BB?"

"Yes, I did."

"More than me? Do you still want her?"

"Could I want the moon more than the sun?"

"Don't give me your slippery, silver tongue—you're not talking to your Senate. God's sake, just answer, did you love her more than me?"

"I loved Betty more than I thought possible—more than myself—but she left me for the three M's—money, money, money. Love to her was a fickle thing. I stopped loving Betty when she stopped being Betty. I never thought I would love again. You have saved my life—I'd die for you." He smiled and mimicked her slight accent. "And *don' blaspheme.*"

"I do *not* speak like that—and I've changed my mind—I love your slippery, silver tongue, shit."

Max smiled. *"Don' swear."*

She smiled confidently. She could see right through Max to his soul. "He will inherit, yes, my son?"

"That again? First, let's get something to inherit, yeah?"

"He will. He must."

"He will."

Cloirina took the child back. Max could see that something was troubling her. "Even if we have a child together?"

"A child? You're gonna be busy, lady—I want more than *a child*, I want a whole bunch of kids."

Cloirina smiled and raised her eyebrows.

Max suddenly made the link. "Hey, you're not?"

"Well …"

"Honey, you're not … are you … pregnant?"

"Maybe … is early days yet, just maybe. But Janus Shar's son—he will be your heir, yes?"

"He's your firstborn. It's your dream, Cloirina. You just let me be in it." His gaze drifted down to her slim waist. "You're certain?"

"I just got over telling you, Maxwell. No, I'm not certain … maybe. Time will tell."

"Yeah, time—time will tell a lot of things."

X

Admiral Keating headed the table in the briefing-room of the aircraft carrier, USS *Hudson*. Max sat with Herman and Onis—they were all decked in uniform, listening intently as Keating explained the proposed battle plan.

"So, gentlemen, that is my Plan A battle strategy … simplicity itself. As a show of kick-ass, we sweep Wesley's fleet out then dump and detonate a shitload of conventional and nuclear ordnance in a line across the Caribbean, one hundred miles in front of him … a kinda "No Entry" sign. Minimum casualties. Neutron leaves no appreciable fallout—just a goddamn motherfucker of a bang. Let the mothers know we're pissed. Any questions?"

The three remained quiet, letting the crude plan sink in.

Onis was the first to speak. "Why the Caribbean, Sir?"

"Why not? There's only two entrances to the canal. You got a better place? Say if you do, Son. This meeting is open for comment. Our base is Panama: left or right, take your pick. You want the Pacific?"

"No, no, no … just thinking aloud."

"Okay. So—"

An aide entered and handed Keating a message. He read it and rolled his eyes. "How in the hell did he get his fleet here so fast?" He handed the paper to Max.

Max glanced at the message. "Does it matter, Admiral?

"Yes, it matters. It means Plan A is out … not enough time."

"The sooner we get to this, the better." Max said. "I say we go out and meet him in deep water. I don't want to destroy any civilian territory."

Keating frowned. "Not such a good idea, Max. What we have to do is use my Plan B. We make the scumbag wait … make him come to us. Gentlemen, we have the canal: if we go through, he'll need to commit half his fleet to follow … then we'll have him like a rat in a pipe."

Hermann raised his hand. "Excuse me, Admiral, Max. I second that. Why don't I take a squad of VTJ's and sink the last ship that follows … right in the canal."

"Yeah! And I'll sink the first," added Onis. "Then half their fleet is fucked. There's a precedent—the Anglo-Dutch War in 1665. The English caught upriver, like, as you say, Admiral, a rat up a pipe. In the Battle of the Medway, the fleet was destroyed at anchor. Jesus, were the English pissed—Samuel Pepys said, 'The Devil shits Dutchmen.' I take that as a compliment … I'm from Dutch parents." He smiled. All looked back stony-faced. He shrugged and continued. "They say it was the blueprint for Pearl Harbor. Anyways, Wesley Shar won't be taking the fight over land. No Sir—too many soft targets."

"Listen to what they're saying, Max," Keating said. "They're making good sense."

"You're wrong—all of you. I'm trying to take these states into the USA. Do I do that by sinking God knows how many nuclear-powered ships in the canal? No way. We take the fight out to sea where it's cleaner. And anyways, he dared come to me—I'll dare go to him."

Onis leapt to his feet. "That's crazy talk! Fuck! We'll be swamped … make him come to you, goddamn it."

Max was seething, but fought against showing it. He knew Keating was right; he knew Onis was right and he knew Hermann was right, but the fact remained. "I won't have a single shell fall on dry land. And that's final. You don't like it—"

Hermann stood and pushed his chair back noisily, "Well, I don't fucking like it."

"Neither do I," said Onis, "and that's a goddamn fact."

"Then don't do it," Max growled. "You're relieved of duty … both of you."

Onis looked to Hermann, and then to Max. Max looked away, showing no quarter. Hermann shrugged and stormed out, followed by Onis.

On the motor launch ferrying them to the escort ship *Electra*, anchored off Cartagena, Onis and Hermann sat solemnly.

"What pissed him?" said Hermann sarcastically.

"The hell do I know? He's got nothing on his mind at the moment … perhaps the Red Sox ain't doing so well."

"They are too! When did your lame-ass team win a World Series?"

"Only last season, smart-ass."

"Oh yeah, go raking up the past, why don't you?"

"Goddamn it, you jerk. You're the wiseass that started this."

"There you go again, raking up the past."

"Nuts!" Onis waved away the stale, idiotic conversation. He shuddered as he contemplated the coming few minutes. "I don't got time for this. You gonna tell her, or what?"

"You tell her … I haven't the heart to do it." He closed his eyes in distaste.

Moments later, on the ship, they faced Cloirina.

"What is it? What's happened? Why are you here?"

"We're relieved of duty!" Hermann said. "And, if he goes out, he is gonna get chewed up and spat out. Damn it, Ma'am, you gotta make him see reason!"

"No! Max will do it his way. Have faith, boys—just a little faith."

Onis shook his head. "To hell with faith—he's gonna get whacked."

XI

From his flagship, *Patriarch*, Wesley Shar surveyed the huge bombardment. Massive flash-flames lit the night sky as his entire fleet fired salvo after salvo. The noise had ceased to be merely deafening—it was now a continuous knot of explosion that, mercifully, his brain had nullified into an almost tangible numbness. It was noise past the point of pain, but to Wesley it was good noise, victorious noise. As he watched, ships on both sides were hit, crippled, and sunk. In the burning sea, sailors awaiting rescue were dying. "If this is what it takes, so be it," he said, hearing his words only in his head against the mayhem of battle. "I am not responsible. I feel no blame. It was not of my doing. It was—"

A vortex of flame cut short his sentence. Wesley found himself on his knees, winded, gasping for breath. His lungs felt like they were solid mass; the flames had all but robbed the deck of oxygen.

Staggering, Wesley looked about him, horrified at the destruction that had been wrought in a matter of seconds. There was a huge hole in the flight deck;

the midship elevator was twisted like molten glass, drooping into the hangar. Deck plates reeled upward in grotesque configurations. Planes stood tail up, belching flame and jet-black smoke.

On the bridge of the *Hudson*, Max also surveyed the battle. His ship had taken three hits, but was still operational. At the helm, Keating peered into a monitor, which displayed Wesley Shar's burning flagship in graphic detail. A glance at the radar placed the two flagships on collision course.

"Holy Mother of God! This is slaughter. We're too close! We can't steer … the rudder is blown away! All I can do is reverse all engines."

"No!" yelled Max as he joined him at the monitor. "Don't you see? We have him! Go for it, Admiral. Ram the bitch! Without Shar, they'll capitulate. Sink that ship and it's over!"

Keating yelled an order to a subordinate, and then turned to Max. "We're sinking ourselves, Max. We got to get off! Our planes can't help us … we're presenting the same target coordinates as the *Patriarch*. We have to move away to give them a chance."

"No!" yelled Max. "Ram speed! Ram speed!"

On the *Electra*, Onis and Hermann watched in horror over the shoulder of the radar operator. Cloirina stood close behind, hands pressed in prayer against her lips.

"Jesus Christ!" Onis cried. "He's heading straight for the center! Of all the stupid—"

Cloirina closed her eyes and sighed. "Max would—that's the only way he knows."

"It'll be okay Ma'am, if he can—"

"It's gone!" yelled Hermann, looking up from the screen. "The *Hudson* is gone!"

Cloirina joined him at the monitor. "Let me see!"

"She was right there just a moment ago, Ma'am."

Cloirina pushed past Hermann and glared into the screen.

"She closed with the *Patriarch*," said Hermann. "Then, then … gone!"

Onis peered into the screen, "Gone? Gone? You mean sunk?"

"In seconds! The magazine must have blown up."

Cloirina wandered around in a daze. "Sunk … sunk?" It didn't sound real; it sounded fanciful, whimsical, impossible. "No, no, no! It can't be! Oh, Max … Max! I'm sorry, so sorry." She sank to her knees. Onis attempted to steady her, but she tumbled onto all fours, unable to control her limbs.

Onis knelt beside her and took her hand. "Ma'am, it don't mean … he could have got off in the boats or a chopper or a jet. It don't mean he's—"

"Dead!" she cried, finishing the word Onis couldn't bring himself to utter. "Dead … Maxwell Tunney! President Tunney is dead. Oh God! How do you say it? Max is … dead!"

Onis helped her to her feet. She bit her hand to calm herself. "We go quickly. We must not be taken. Max would not have wanted that."

Hermann shook his head. "No, not yet. We're not sure who has the day, Ma'am."

"We've lost!" Cloirina said. "Without Max, we cannot win. Max made a mistake—he should have made them come to us. Give the order to go back to Port Cartagena."

From the air, the two ships resembled an illuminated T plucked from the cross-row of an ancient alphabet; drawn in radiating spirals of fiery reds, graphic grays, and glistering golds. The two great ships were spliced together like a seaman's knot—the *Hudson* across the bow of the *Patriarch*, highlighted in fire.

On the bridge of the *Hudson*, Max scrutinized the carnage, trying to evaluate the life expectancy of his ship. The bow was rammed into the belly of the other ship and both were sinking.

"Max!" Keating yelled. "We have to move! We got to try to break away and ram the bitch again—then abandon ship! Max!"

"Okay, okay!" said Max. He jolted into action. "Reverse engines then set to ram! Give the order to lower the boats. We do this right, we've won."

The ship began to groan as its nuclear engine started to tug it free of the *Patriarch*. Max grabbed the radio officer. "Get a message to the *Electra*. Message to read—"

"Sir," interrupted the operator. "The *Electra* is not answering. I think our antenna is down. I have it on radar, but it seems to be moving out of the battle zone! The fleet is going back, Sir."

Max gave a look of amazement, "Back? Back? I don't believe it!"

"We don't have time, Mr. President," yelled Keating. "We need to launch all VTJs then abandon ship. I repeat, launch all aircraft and abandon ship! You must give the order; we have to ram again. Max!"

"Back? Something's happened. She's been hit. I have to go to her."

"No, Max!" Keating yelled. "You have to give the order, damn it!"

Max ran from the bridge and dashed out onto the flight deck—flame and explosions all around him. He stumbled through the smoke toward the one remaining jump jet.

The VTJ was ready, flaming up for takeoff as Max clambered onto the wing. He ordered the co-pilot out and climbed inside the cockpit. He donned a flight helmet and yelled over the intercom. "Get us out of here, now! Find the *Electra*." The pilot hesitated and was about to comment. Max screamed, "Get going—that's an order!"

"Aye, aye, Sir! I have her on screen."

"Can you contact her?"

"Negative, Sir. All radio messages relay through the ship's decoder, but that's down. I could contact our Colombia base."

"No! Close in. We're going to land on her."

Beneath his helmet, the pilot looked astonished. "The *Electra* has no VTJ landing facility, Sir, just a cluttered main-deck, and she's under full power … Sir."

"Can it be done?"

The pilot smiled, contemplating the dangerous prospect. "Aye, aye, Sir! You betcha … Sir!"

Max leaned back in his seat and left the pilot to concentrate on takeoff. The craft rose like a rocket, straight up through the smoke of battle into clear, clean air. At a thousand feet, it leveled off and flew straight ahead. In the distance, Max could just make out the *Electra*. From this height, the deck seemed impossibly small, cluttered with hatches, cables, and the apparatus of war.

The distance quickly closed and the VTJ made a pass over the ship. "Sir!" said the pilot. "I'm going around one more time. I need to gain currency with the pitch of the ship."

"Do what you have to, Son. Just get us down."

The pilot made another pass, perilously close to the forward mast, attempting to match the speed, pitch, and roll of the ship. The aircraft yawed away, narrowly avoiding the steel forest of aerials and radar housings. The pilot attempted a landing; the ship suddenly lurched, thrusting up toward the VTJ. The engines screamed and it rammed into the sky, narrowly avoiding crashing into the deck.

On the bridge, Onis stared into the scanner while Hermann feverishly tinkered with the radio, searching for a contact.

Hermann called out to Onis, "No verbal contact from the incoming jet, but its chip is emitting scan-friendly code."

"What the hell? The *Hudson* ... she's back on screen!" He leaped to his feet and danced around, whooping and cheering. He hugged Hermann and planted a slobbering kiss on his forehead. "The *Hudson* is back!"

"The hell you on, boy?" Hermann growled as he pulled away, wiping his face in disgust.

"Look!" yelled Onis, roughly swinging him around to face the monitor.

"Well, I'll be! It's there! The fucker's there!"

"It must have been locked together with the *Patriarch*," said Onis. "Quick, man, go tell Cloirina that we're turning back to the battle zone."

From the bridge, Hermann saw the jump jet coming in to make another pass on the ship. "Goddamn, that pilot must be crazy. No way in hell he'll put that thing down … he'll have to ditch in the sea."

The jet closed; again the ship lurched. This time, the pilot matched the rhythm of the sea, anticipating the dip and roll. The deck rose again and the pilot trimmed the thrusts. Ship and aircraft came together in a tremendous skidding crash. Defying belief, the aircraft was on the cluttered deck in one piece. Immediately, seamen rushed out to tether it to the deck. Max scrambled out and made for the main cabin.

A petty officer entered and saluted Onis. "Sir, a VTJ has just landed on deck."

"The hell it has!" Onis gasped in amazement.

"Sir, it's the President."

"Tunney?" Hermann yelled in disbelief.

"Yes, Sir. President Tunney, Sir … he's just landed." The officer stepped aside as Hermann rushed past him. Onis pushed past the officer and followed, catching up Hermann as he tore open the door of Cloirina's cabin. Max was already there—in Cloirina's arms.

"Max!" yelled Onis. "What in hell's happened?"

"It's over! The *Hudson* is finished. She's gone. We rammed the *Patriarch* and—"

"No, Sir," Hermann said. "The *Hudson* is safe—it's the *Patriarch* that's sinking."

Max looked aghast, hardly understanding. He turned to Cloirina. "But you were leaving."

"I thought you were dead. They …" she glanced at Hermann, "they said you were dead."

Hermann returned her glance and then turned back to Max. "Dear God, Max. The whole fleet is following— they're all returning. We've lost the day!"

Max covered his face with his hands as the awful truth of what he had caused to happen finally registered.

XII

Max had eaten virtually nothing in the weeks following the defeat. He wandered aimlessly through the gardens of the Jade Palace, his only nourishment being coffee, whisky, and more whisky. No matter how much he drank, he could not claim a single moment's respite from the nightmare. He was Napoleon after Waterloo, blaming everyone and everything in its turn, but always coming back to his own weakness, his love and utter dependence on Cloirina.

Alone in the gardens of the Jade Palace, he stared despondently into space. Onis and Hermann stood some distance away, studying his deeply depressed face.

Onis shook his head wearily. "I'm worried about him … he's not coming out of this … there's things he's got to do."

Hermann shrugged. "Yeah, yeah. Well, I'm worried about you and me. How do we come out of this?"

Onis considered a moment. "Not too well, I'm afraid, old buddy—but not as bad as Keating."

"Yeah. I reckon. Keating has half the fleet battle-station ready. There is no other way for him … treason carries the death penalty for him."

"For us all … Jesus." The two men slowly walked toward the virtual comatose Max.

"Cloirina?" said Onis. "How's she handling all this?"

Hermann shrugged. "To hell with Cloirina! She don't figure in my list of favorite people at this moment. She started this. Cloirina can do what Cloirina does best—look out for her goddamn self!"

Onis put his fingers to his closed eyes in despair. "You think Max is up to it? Is he game for another fight?"

"No! I don't think so—not in his present mood. He thinks he's a beaten man. You think it'll come to that?"

"Yeah, it'll come to that. All Max wants is to feel someone's fist in his face. He tried to pick a fight with me yesterday. Called me a coward because I wouldn't shape up with him."

"No kidding?"

"Yeah! No kidding? I wish I had. As I say, he just wants to feel someone's fist. I think he feels he needs it … or something."

"Well, he'd better not try it on with me—I might just fucking oblige him. Hey, hush up, he's watching us."

Max rubbed his hands roughly over his face, pulled himself together, and wandered over to meet them.

"Max, Mr. President," said Onis, trying a jovial tilt to his voice. "How goes it?"

Hermann nodded his greeting.

Max studied his two thuggish minders for a long, uncomfortable moment. "Let me tell you guys something about being a Senator, Vice President, and a President. You learn to be devious. You learn to look out for yourself. You learn tricks—get it … tricks? You learn to read papers on other people's desks, sideways and upside-down. You learn to read what people are writing just by watching the pen in their hand move." He diverted his stare into Hermann's face. "And you also learn to read people's fucking lips!"

With these words still in the air, Max loosed an inspired right hook, catching Hermann smack on the side of his chin and knocking him backward into Onis' arms.

The hint of a smile on Max's face was the first in over a week. He stood like a boxer—hands up, ready to fight. "I'd be 'obliged' Sir," said Max with antiquated relish. "If you would follow through. And I will oblige you by allowing you a reciprocal, undefended punch."

Hermann gathered himself. "That's quite a dig you have, Sir, but I'll decline if you don't mind. I'm not in the murdering vein today."

"Come on—you can get all that I-told-you-so, I-said-this-would-happen, You-should-have-listened-to-me out of your system. Come on! I can see it in your eyes. You're saying it behind my back—say it to my face. Come on!"

Max lurched drunkenly toward Hermann. Onis stepped between. Max threw him a glancing jab, which was easily parried.

"Woo! Hold off there, Max, you're hitting your old amigos here."

"Then let's go on the town," said Max as he spun around from the inertia of the missed blow. "Let's tie one on, *amigos!*"

"I don't think Cloirina will like that too much, Max," said Hermann, trying his best to curb his anger.

"To hell with Cloirina—she ain't talking to me, anyways. Either you come with me or I go on my own … and you know what happens when I do that. What will Cloirina say if she knows you let me out on my own to get beat up again?"

Onis steadied Max. "That won't happen anymore, Mr. President. Every dive in town has been warned off. You won't pick a fight nowhere in the whole of Brazil."

"You wanna bet? Come on—I know a place. Either that or I'll fight you both—here and now. What do you say … we won't tell Cloirina … what do ya say, boys? The Three Amigos—one for all and all for me. Remember Vegas?"

Onis let Max go. He was steadier now, but still had a wild look in his eyes. Max meant to have trouble—he required it like an addict craving a fix. He needed his fix and Hermann and Onis were his only connection.

Onis sighed in defeat. "Okay, okay—but Vegas was light years ago, Max. We'll go, but you wear a stab vest. Yeah?"

"We all wear vests," growled Hermann.

Max smiled wickedly. "Wear what you goddamn like—let's get it on. I know a place, out of town: Recife. I learned to dance the ciranda there—in front of the little white church in Boa Viagem. Fire up the chopper."

They arrived just after the evening mass and the weather couldn't have been better. Already a great crowd had gathered. In the town center, people of all ages held hands and formed a large circle. The steps were very simple and the rhythm was slow and hypnotic, going round and round, the music rhythms changing periodically, a cue for the circle to change direction. In a ciranda, people can come in and leave as they please, and the dance goes on all night long, with people eating and drinking *batidas* and *cachaça*, a potent drink made from fermented sugarcane mixed with tropical fruit juices.

As Max and his entourage entered the square, the small band—made up of brass and drums, and a male singer—wove a rendering of the "Star Spangled Banner" into their song. The hope of anonymity, it seemed, was blown.

"Jesus!" said Max. "How in hell they get to know … we only just decided?"

"Guess they might have got a clue when they gave us landing instructions," said Hermann with a hint of sarcasm. "You know—being the Presidential air code, an all."

"Goddamn it! You asked for landing instructions? Why?"

"Oh, I don't know—maybe I didn't fancy doing a fucking Pooley. You know what I'm saying?"

"Fuck Pooley. Fuck you. Fuck Brazil—and fuck everything else. I'm going for some fun!"

Max turned and dashed into the crowd. Fortunately for him, most of the people had not realized what was happening and they opened up to let him pass. Onis and Hermann followed close on his heels. When they caught up, Max had acquired a *carimbo*, a huge drum of African origin, made of a hollow tree-trunk section and covered with deerskin.

With some degree of force, Max had loutishly snatched the drum from its owner—a small, and now extremely angry, middle-aged Brazilian man, who was desperately trying to retrieve it. Max was paying him no heed, gratuitously smashing the drum with a whisky bottle as a drumstick. When Onis arrived, he attempted to pry the instrument free. Max was having none of it—he shrieked and whooped with laughter, bashing the drum even harder until the drum skin burst. Max threw the broken instrument back to the irate owner, and then turned to move on.

The little man grabbed at Max, hurling a barrage of unintelligible insults. Max, finding it all too amusing, stopped the man with a short jab to the jaw. The punch was purposely not hard, but sharp enough to infuriate the man into action, comprising of two sharp hooks, one either side of Max's temple. Then Hermann was on him, winding the little man's arms up behind his back.

Max had got what he'd wanted, the two punches had the sting of passion, but not—he hoped—the power to bruise. Hermann peeled off a more-than-required compensatory wad of notes, and thrust them under the little man's nose and then into his hands. This served only to refuel the man's anger. He struggled to get to Max, and it was only after Hermann waved his pistol in his face that he reluctantly backed off.

After the man had calmed slightly, Onis let him go. Max studied him as he turned away and looked at his broken drum. He then looked at the handful of money, seemingly mesmerized by the wad of crisp American banknotes. He looked again at his drum, peeled off a few dollars, and threw the rest at Max's feet. He then walked off with the remnant of his instrument tucked caringly under his arm.

"Well," said Onis. "That went well. Anything else you want to get out of your system?"

Max was lost in thought; he couldn't for the life of him understand why the little man had thrown away so much money—possibly a year's salary—supposing the man was fortunate enough to have a job. "Why? Why?" Max already knew the answer.

"Hey, Doodle Dandy," said Onis. "You hear what I'm saying? Anything else?"

Max gathered himself and brushed off his clothes. "We got to get back," he said as he attempted to straighten his hair. "I got a drum that needs fixing."

In the palace library, Cloirina sat alone, staring into a CCT monitor. The Senate was in progress. Walter Braganza, now looking old and feeble, addressed the riotous assembly. He had to shout over the din to be heard.

"We must move onward—there's no going back. We have taken a monumental step forward, and prosperity can be the only outcome: prosperity for North, Middle, and South America ... The Americas. Together they are far bigger than a few overambitious players."

One Senator stood and shouted above the rest. "Where is Tunney? Why isn't he here? He should be here. Where is Tunney?"

The house picked up his chant. "Where is Tunney? Where is Tunney?

Cloirina switched off the TV. Max had entered while she'd been absorbed in her uncle's ineffectual address, and he now stood beside her.

"It's okay, Max. They hit out at everything and everyone—it is their way. They'll come around. Money, in the end, will talk."

"You think so?"

"Oh, yes. Now the people have had a taste of first-world living, they will not want to give it up … and the North still wants territory. We must play out our hand, Maxwell. Max! Are you listening?"

Max wearily pressed his fingers to his closed eyes. "Yeah, yeah, I'm listening." He leaned across her and switched the monitor back on. On the screen, Walter continued addressing the house.

"—Yes, I hear what you are saying. The United European peace delegation has made yet another plea to Shar. They want to extend the cease-fire. Further, in the event of Washington's continued recalcitrance, the ASEAN delegation is ready to enter the peace arena."

A second Senator shouted from the assembly, "Is there to be an invasion?"

"No! There will be no invasion," Walter snapped. "That talk is pure fantasy."

"Not fantasy … reality!" The Senator's voice grew angry. "America is here already— Tunney. If we resist, the United States, under Wesley Shar, it'll be Guerra de las Malvinas, Vietnam, Iraq all over again. America won't negotiate while Tunney is here. We want him out!" He chanted, "Out! Out! Out!" He waved his hands for his colleagues to join in. Walter screamed for order, but the House picked up the chant. "Out! Out! Out!"

Max switched off the TV. Cloirina stood to take his arm and led him to the French windows. "We must greet our people, Max," she said with a strained smile.

They stood silently for a moment and studied the mob through the closed windows.

Onis entered. "Shall we hear them properly?" he said to Max. "Shall I open the doors?"

Max looked at his watch. "No, not yet. Put the TV back on—there's a news bulletin due."

Onis switched it on and stood aside. "You going to watch, Max?"

"No, just turn up the sound. I'll listen from here."

Onis adjusted the volume. "Here it comes." The camera closed in on the newscaster.

"In neutral Cuba today, the United European peace delegation made a further plea to Washington to end hostilities toward the newly formed USSA—the Unified States of Southern America. All that was achieved was a forty-eight-hour extension of the cease-fire. We now cross over to Sir Rupert Llewellyn, in Havana."

The TV image cut to the UE peace envoy on a studio set. Sir Rupert Llewellyn, a distinguished looking man with graying temples, stood before a cluster of microphones, surrounded by bustling reporters.

"Will there be war?"

"The cease-fire, Sir Rupert, will it stand?"

"Will Wesley Shar attack the mainland?"

Llewellyn raised a hand, momentarily quelling the questions. "I'm afraid Wesley Shar is unshakeable. His terms, as re-submitted by the Senate, are unchanged: All American rebels under Maxwell Tunney and all American service personnel under the command of Admiral Keating will be given amnesty and immunity from prosecution and court-martial, if—"

A burst of frenzied voices drowned him out.

"If Shar wins, will he rule The Americas?"

"Will Shar deal with Brazil or Argentina?"

"Will Shar be *Presidente*?"

Llewellyn raised his hands and continued. "—If they lay down their arms and present themselves to a UN marshal within the next forty-eight hours … the duration of the cease-fire. I'm sorry, ladies and gentlemen, but there the communication ends." He turned away, offering no more comment to the mob of reporters, who continued to shout their questions.

The TV cut back to the newscaster.

"It is further reported that the US fleet, under direct command of Wesley Shar, has grown twofold in the last twenty-four hours, and that several military divisions have massed at the US-Mexico border in readiness for a land invasion." He glanced down at an open laptop on the news-desk, and then back to the camera. "News just at hand reports that the ASEAN delegation has arrived in Havana and will meet later today with the US ambassador. That concludes this news bulletin. Next update at—"

Onis switched off the TV and looked to Max for comment. Max shrugged. "What you get is what you get. What did Keating say?"

Onis looked uneasy. "Keating was somewhat pissed that you ever doubted him."

Max looked aghast. "Damn it, Onis. I never doubted him! You should have made that clear. I just wanted to remove the burden of loyalty from his own judgment—for him to offer his personnel the chance to capitulate. What's he thinking of? Doubt?"

"Keating's with us, Mr. President, '200 percent'—his words."

Max slowly walked to the window, indicating the crowd outside. "And them?"

Onis shrugged. "Why not ask them? Will you address them, Ma'am?"

Cloirina gave Onis a withering look. "We will both address them. Won't we, Max?"

Max reluctantly nodded.

Cloirina took his arm as they stood before the balcony windows. "Another fine mess I got us into, yes? Come, *Meester Presiden,* our people want to throw eggs at us. We don't want to disappoint them."

Cloirina was radiant, despite the fact that her world was tumbling about her oh-so-pretty shoulders. Max shook his head in admiration. *What a piece of work,* he thought. *Some piece of work.*

He shrugged and pulled himself to his full height. He placed his hand on Cloirina's arm, opened the doors, and together they strode majestically onto the balcony. As they stepped out, the crowd hushed—and then a mighty cheer swelled up.

"Americas! Americas! Americas!"

Trying to hide his astonishment, Max took hold of Cloirina's hand, raising it to the adoring multitude.

"Cloirina! Cloirina! Cloirina!"

Cloirina now took Max's arm, lifting it as high as she could.

The chant reverted back to, "Americas! Americas! Americas!"

XII

Max stood alone, addressing the Select Committee of the Brazilian Upper House. After the proletariat's hearty vote of confidence, Max's depression had lifted somewhat. The people had given him another chance, but now he had to convince the money.

"I have put my claim to sole presidency to the UN International Court of Justice. And, as you are aware, they can find no impeachable transgression. What I have done is totally in accordance with both international law and the American Constitution. However..." He let the word hang as he looked around. Every member waited spellbound for him to continue. Their avarice was palpable. Some were sweating and some jabbered nervously to confederates. Some sat staring, not daring to miss a word. Max played their tension as if stroking a fishing line; the fish were nibbling, but hadn't quite swallowed the hook.

"However," he repeated the word for effect, "the same is so with Wesley Shar's sole presidency claim.

In short, we have somewhat of a paradox." As Max sat down, the nervous mumblings rose.

Now Walter Braganza stood. He bowed to the speaker, and after being given the nod to speak, raised his hands dramatically. "As premier of Brazil, I speak for the people. They do not want to lose what they have gained. We don't need a referendum to know that—and there is no time for such luxury. But the people are afraid. If Maxwell Tunney falls, then Brazil alone will be the scapegoat—and it will be with Argentina that The Americas will consummate." He turned and directed his words to Max. "We, Brazil—your resolute partner—need assurances."

The old man sat down to silence.

Max waited a few moments, and then slowly rose to his feet. He folded his arms across his chest in a show of proud confidence. "As President of Lower, Middle and Upper America, and Canada, I can give you my word—I give Brazil my word—Brasilia will be the Constantinople of the New World: bonding governments, people, and church together into The Americas." *Were they ready? Maybe, maybe not quite yet.* "There will be no invasion—I have offered to fight Shar in the ballot box."

There were mumblings and gestures of approval. Encouraged, Max slightly raised his voice. "When Wesley Shar predicted that he and I would stand toe-to-toe, he failed to predict the outcome, whereas I can predict ... I have the people, the Holy Catholic Church, and the whole Western world behind me. But above all, I have Cloirina Braganza and Brazil! Can a cause have all this and not prevail?" He yelled these last words like a battle cry. The whole house cheered … they had swallowed, bait, hook, and line.

XIV

From the bridge of the USS *Hudson*, Admiral Keating surveyed the bustle of activity as the great ship underwent repairs and refit. He carried a look of torment as he watched his personnel make ready for the battle he knew must come ... the unthinkable, civil war ... a hellish, ignoble thing. But he was a soldier and—

The intercom buzzed, interrupting his troubled thoughts. He snatched it up and barked into the mouthpiece. "Yes! ... Who? What in hell does he want? Okay, bring him to the bridge." He slammed the handset down, put his hand to his face, and held his jaw in contemplation. After a few moments, an aide entered.

"Okay," said Keating. "Wheel him in."

The aide stepped back and an officer entered and saluted.

Keating saluted back, and then turned to the aide. "Leave us... no interruptions." The aide saluted and left.

"Okay. What's on your mind? And make it quick, I don't got time for no bullshit."

In the silver light of the waxing moon, Max and Cloirina were motionless in each other's arms on the great, four-poster bed.

"So," said Cloirina. "Will he stoop and pick up the gauntlet?"

They were in the splendid master bedroom of the Hacienda Caimito, a picturesque chateau seventy-five miles inland from Port Cartagena and his anchored battle fleet. Max was thoughtful. If Wesley went to the ballot box, Max would undoubtedly win. It would take many months of campaigning—and he knew Wesley could not keep his dubious character in check and away from public scrutiny for that period of time. People just didn't like him. 'I'm unlikable' were his own words.

"Will he go to the ballot box?" said Cloirina, lying naked across his chest.

"No, damn him, he won't risk a democratic vote. He don't need to, it seems."

"So … there will be another battle?"

"Oh, yes," said Max with a touch of irony. "I always knew there would be. They want my blood. There is no other way now—he has the Shar, three M's machine on his side."

"Can we win such a war … we don't have the resources?"

"Yes, we can win! We are putting world order under threat—that, and the fact that everyone wants part of The Americas action. Russia is demanding a voice— separate from Eurasia—they back us. The English and French, understandably, want to remain neutral, but the EU will not accept their veto. Australia and New Zealand are at each other's throats. New Zealand backs us and they've got the whole goddamn Pacific siding with them. World order is under threat—that's what we play on. We're rocking the planet, literally!"

Cloirina gave a look of horror. "World War III?"

"No. No! If I thought that, why I'd ..."

"You'd what, Max?"

"No, not World War III, I don't think that for a single God-sent second. We need just one battle, one almighty bombardment. We throw everything conventional and nuclear—all or nothing—Keating's original Plan A, to detonate half our entire ordnance in the Caribbean Sea, in a five-hundred-mile line across the exclusion zone—a show of force. Keating's calling it the Tunney Line."

"Dear God, forgive me! Max, what have I done?"

He pulled her close. "Don't worry. As I say, it's a show of force: minimum casualties, the biggest man-made explosion the world has ever seen or heard, and a short-life radiation curtain drawn across the canal. But they must start it. Just one warning shot, one missile-lock, and ... Armageddon! When world order and the American public see the devastation that just one bombardment can deliver, Shar will be forced to the ballot box ... and we've won."

"And if he doesn't?"

Max was searching for a reply when Cloirina suddenly covered his mouth with a kiss, stifling his words.

XV

Wesley Shar's fleet was under full steam. Wesley stood on the bridge of the convoy leader, USS *Lexington*. Looking over the radar operator's shoulder, he was grim-faced.

Meanwhile, Max Tunney entered the crowded control center of his flagship, the *Braganza*. His mood was quite different—he felt full of life, full of optimism. His fleet idled off of Cartagena. Max did not expect an engagement, but he was there, ready—effectively blockading the Caribbean entrance to the canal. However, Max's buoyant disposition was to prove short-lived as Onis' face of doom greeted him.

"Sure you're up to this, boy?" Max demanded, ignoring his disagreeable look.

"Bad news, Mr. President."

Max sighed. "How bad?"

Onis realized that this would destroy Max, but there was no easy way. "Bad, bad news."

Max sighed again. "Okay, give."

"Hermann—behind my back—brokered a deal with Keating. Acting for him, he's won amnesty with Shar. Keating won't be a player today."

Max momentarily closed his eyes, accepting the inevitable. In his mind's eye, he visualized the tumultuous barrage that Keating was to have provided: a barely credible flash of white light; a massive explosion ripping open the heavens; contrails of conflagration dancing one hundred miles, producing a swath of fire leaping from the sea up into the stratosphere; a thunderous knot of explosions enough to rupture the unprotected ear; the horrendous shockwave creeping across the no-man's-land of ocean; the whirlwind, heralding the juggernaut, pyroclastic wave of destruction on those who resisted— and the subsequent capitulation.

Max opened his eyes and surveyed the calm sea.

Onis now stood in front of Max, blocking his view. "You okay, Mr. President?"

Max shrugged, "I guess." He peered past Onis to the horizon, to Wesley's distant fleet, just in time to see the powder-flash as the *Lexington* opened fire. "So it begins."

It seemed an eternity before they heard the report of the guns.

Onis smiled. "Yeah, nothing like a good broadside to blow away the cobwebs."

A low whistle … and then a high-pitched whine as the first barrage fell short.

Max gathered himself. "Onis, get all aircraft aloft. You take the last VTJ … you have command now. Get all our ships out of the line of fire and take them back to Port Cartagena."

"Sir? What about you?"

"The *Braganza* stays … they need something to engage. I stay as rear-guard while the fleet withdraws."

"But what about *you?*"

Ignoring the question, Max picked up the intercom. As he yelled into the handset, the second barrage began. "Now hear this: lower all boats and prepare to abandon ship! Repeat! Lower all boats and leave the ship immediately! Out."

There was a shuddering explosion as the *Braganza* took a direct hit. A flash-flame tore through the ship, sending men and aircraft crashing into the sea. Max, Onis, and the subordinate officers on the bridge staggered under the tremendous shockwave. Max just managed to stay upright.

Onis had fallen, but was now climbing to his feet. "What about you?" he yelled across the smoke-filled bridge.

"I'm staying. Onis, you've been my one faithful friend and ally, don't go spoiling it! I'm staying."

"Aye, aye, Mr. President, I understand. I'll carry out your orders to the letter."

"Then get your ass into gear! Now!"

Onis didn't move. "No message for Cloirina?"

"Nothing that's worth putting into mere words … she'll understand. Now go!"

Another salvo of shells exploding around the *Braganza* set off a frenzy of onboard activity. Boats were lowered on the lee side. Aircraft lifted off, banking sharply south, to head for home. Onis prepared the last remaining VTJ.

When Max was satisfied that all personnel had abandoned ship, he quickly made his way to the reactor room. He disarmed the first two barriers and moved on to the third: a high-strength compartment within which the all-welded primary system and nuclear reactor were located: a compartment to hold back the release of any primary coolant system liquid or pressure leakage. Max bypassed this system with a double set of keys, followed by fingerprint-scan and retina recognition. Immediately a warning klaxon sounded—a low bleep gradually rising to a continuous wail as the fuel rods started to emerge deep from their mica-concrete protective housings. Max stripped off his uniform and stood naked in front of the rising rods. He stood in silhouette against the red warning lights, allowing the deadly rays to penetrate his body.

Onis' voice boomed out over the intercom. "Max, the Klaxons are sounding! What the hell you doing?"

Max's head sunk into his hands. "Onis! You disobeyed my direct order."

"That order is carried out, Mr. President, to the letter. Our fleet is entering the canal. Come away now, Sir. You've soaked up enough radiation to take out a whole state."

"Not yet."

"Fuck this! I'm coming to get you."

"No!"

The intercom went dead.

Onis entered the reactor room wearing a red radiation suit and transparent dome helmet and carrying another under his arm. He started to retract the rods.

"Get away," Max screamed. "You're killing yourself!"

"Then *you* come away. We have to shut the reactor down, Max, we're sinking!"

"Okay, but back off—now! Don't get near me, Onis. I'm deadly. I can't leave here."

"The hell you can. You didn't believe I would leave you, did you, Max? I got you a suit … if it can keep radiation out, it can keep it in. I'm taking you to the Hacienda Caimito—to Cloirina. You don't get to die alone in this shit-hole. Now, don't argue with me—or we both finish it here."

Max put up no fight as Onis helped him into the suit. "You'll take me to her?" he whispered. "You'd do that for me?"

"Sure I would, Max. You feeling okay?"

"Oh, just, doodle dandy, Onis…… just doodle…" Max sunk to his knees.

On the battered flight deck, amid flames and explosions, Onis struggled to carry Max to a waiting jump jet, and then up into the cockpit. After a few moments, the jet gracefully lifted off, circled the ship once, and then flew toward the shore at full speed. From the cockpit canopy, Max was cheered to see the *Braganza's* lifeboats making for the coast, the last of them safely sheltered by the huge bulk of the doomed ship. When they had reached halfway, the *Braganza* exploded in an immense plume of fire and smoke.

Her stern lifted and she started to slip slowly into the burning ocean.

The VTJ landed safely in the Hacienda Caimito grounds. The moment it touched down, Cloirina ran to meet it—oblivious to the dust and grass blowing into her face. The engines died and Onis helped Max, his helmet visor now streaked with sweat and vomit, into Cloirina's waiting arms.

Onis tried to keep her at a distance, but she resisted. "Keep back, Ma'am. He's highly radioactive. He's lethal. You can't go near him without a suit. I got you a suit. Tell everybody here to keep away."

"They've all gone. We are completely alone. I sent them away. They've taken my son to Argentina."

Onis grabbed her shoulders. "Jesus Christ, what are we going to do? He's—"

"Dying," Max said. "And nothing on this Earth can stop it." He turned to Cloirina and smiled weakly. "Sorry, I meant to go down with my ship. I cheated it once—seems the sea just don't want me."

Max was now sleeping in the big four-poster bed. Cloirina and Onis stood by his side—all three were in radiation suits.

Onis sighed and turned to Cloirina. "He's got about three-quarters of an hour … I think. It won't be painful … he'll just go to sleep."

She blew Max a kiss through her glass dome and then looked at Onis. The big man had tears in his eyes. "There's nothing more you can do, Onis. You must go and save yourself. I'll look after him now."

Onis attempted to push the tears back across his temples with finger and thumb, but all he touched was the glass dome of his helmet. He gave a deep sigh as the tears rolled down his cheeks. "He's the best man I ever knew. He was my friend and he was my President. I salute him." He stood at attention and saluted solemnly.

"And you were the truest friend he ever had." Cloirina grasped his gloved hand. "I thank you for being there for him. Please, make sure they look after my son."

Onis looked at her, suddenly understanding. "I guess I'll be going now, Ma'am. God be with you both." He turned and moved off.

Through the window, she watched him thoroughly hose down his radiation suit before climbing into the VTJ. After a few moments, the aircraft rose into the sky and away.

As Max slept, Cloirina removed his suit and washed him. She sat watching over him.

After a moment, Max opened his eyes. He saw her and smiled. He then realized he was naked. "Hey, where's my suit?"

"It looked uncomfortable; I took it off. How you feeling, Max?"

Max forced a smile. "Radiant!"

"Bad joke, Maxwell. Four Hail Mary's."

"Sorry, Honey ... this way is clean. There really was no other way."

She nodded agreement. His eyes started to flicker and she touched his brow tenderly. "Close your eyes, Darling, just for a moment."

"Yeah, you got to move away from me. It's too dangerous—even in your suit … the baby. Go while I sleep a little. You'll wake me in a while … promise? You won't just let me go?"

"In a while, I promise."

Max closed his eyes. She looked down at him and smiled tenderly. "If I had just one day left on earth and I could spend it with you, I'd think myself lucky." She started to strip off her own radiation suit and then removed her underclothes. When she was naked, she pulled away the sheets. Max was sleeping. As she climbed in beside him, he momentarily opened his eyes and smiled. She kissed him, held him, and pulled him to her.

Through the window, the sun arced rapidly across the afternoon sky and on into twilight, into evening, and into night. The moon took its place and the stars trailed beside.

The dawn brought the sound of helicopters. The noise of their rotors slowed to a low drone, and then to a deep throb, and then stopped. Silence.

In the White House, the mood was of nervous, highly cautious jubilation. All parties had requested a State-of-the-Nation summit, which was now in progress.

Wesley Shar stood majestic at the lectern; he made no attempt at the macho image he had proffered in the Tri-Presidency era. His subordinate generals and handpicked Senators sat in a semi-circle around him; he could feel their avarice burning in the back of his neck. There would be no democratic re-election. As sole surviving President of The Americas, there was no one to deny him. He raised a hand and the whole Senate rose to their feet in homage. One empire falls, another rises. One *emperor* falls—.